The Rainbow Connection

Herman U. Ticz

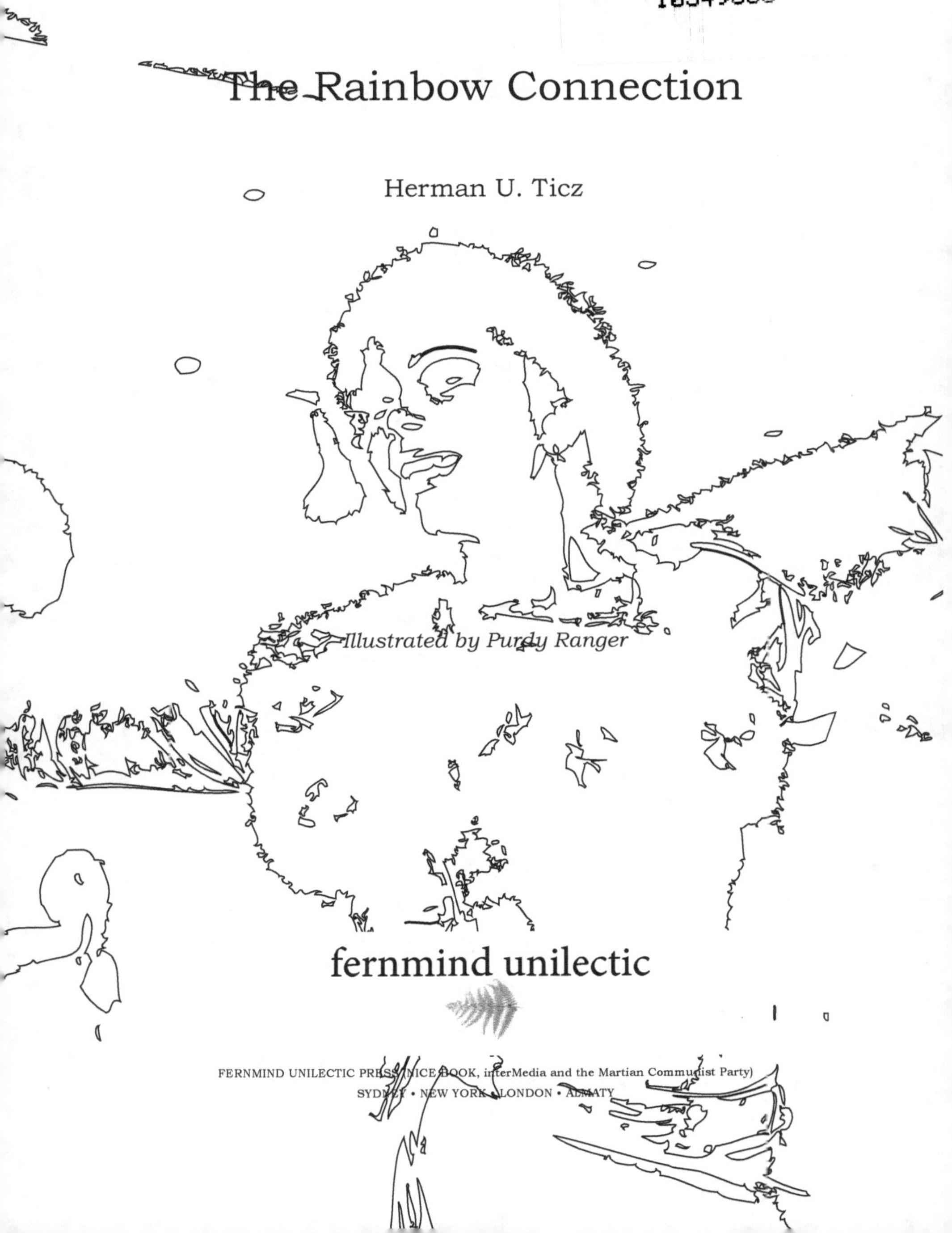

Illustrated by Purdy Ranger

fernmind unilectic

FERNMIND UNILECTIC PRESS (NICE BOOK, interMedia and the Martian Commudist Party)
SYDNEY • NEW YORK • LONDON • ALMATY

KIDS CAN'T STOP READING
THE DETERMINE YOUR OWN DEVIATION™ STORIES!

"It begins as a detective novel, dips before long into screwball comedy, and at its close – when the dead speak – becomes a tale of possession." – Cary Romanos, age 12

"Right now, no writer – reporter or novelist – is getting [the Zeitgeist] on paper better than Mr. Ticsz." – Pvd. Q. Q Arnie–Adams, The Wall Street Journal, age 11

"A masterpiece ... the difference between seeing the world in slices and seeing it in the fullest spectrum of a sun–shower rainbow ... rainbow connected that is ... " – Andrew Ferguson, The Daily Freak, age 9

"Makes you think thoroughly before making decisions. Deviations is dope!" – Hassan Stevenson, age 11

And the teachers like this series, too:

"This book contains all the topics required for the 'common core' of the Certificate of Junior High Education in the Metaeducation. Each of the topics has been dealt with in a simple, yet concise fashion." – Dr. Ewen Wesi, Southern Invisible College, Melbourne.

DETERMINE YOUR OWN DEVIATION™
AND MAKE READING MORE FUN!

For information address: Fernmind Unilectic Prose, Inc., just down the lane by the pool of reflection and tree of understanding.

Published simultaneously in the United States, Australia, the Republic of Kazakhstan, the Ancient Land of Albion and the Wastes of Martian HQ.

Authorized by the Martian Communist Party. Propaganda certified by the Verandah Vanguard.

Watch out for these titles coming up in the Determine Your Own Deviation™ series.

Ask your bookseller for books you have missed or visit us at fernmind.com to learn more.

203. Transylvanian rapture
204. Penge–twiddle umpteen voluptuous the third and the inauthentic bandits of the chasm
205. John Dee goes bananas in Hypersalafiland
206. Chakra Rabbit versus the Cosmic Bride

If you are interested in learning more about the Truth, perhaps you might care to peruse other Fernmind titles:

The Doctrine of Desmond
The Rise and Fall of the Cyborgwittgenstein
Malcontented discharge of the Sign of the Party

The distant future.

The Republic of the Martian Communist Revolution rules the continent of Eurasia according to the principles of Evolutionary Social Dynamism, a Theologico–Darwinian–Marxist assemblage espoused by the Great Cyborgwittgenstein, the (now usurped) first President of the State of Truth. Its principles were first laid down by that Magnificent Tailor of the Design in his *Manifesto for the Verandah Vanguard*:

> We proclaim the intrinsic Divinity of elevated evolution in all things, godly growth, managed mutation, righteous revolution, running through all areas of society like bifircating lines of electric fire, predicating upon all interpretations of the social, from the communities that comprise the human psyche, to family units and love affairs and philosophies and sciences, to the entire geo–politics of the State itself. Everything is in fluent flux, everything is permitted, life is a laboratory and we are chemists in experimentation: but with the Goal that, ultimately, each experiment across all levels leads us closer to a Perfection that permeates through all levels. Through continual flux is perfection's derivation, true social evolution. Previous revolutions failed because they did not take into account *constant* mental revolution is required for there to be progress: not a single political moment, but a continual struggle within the ummatic assembly of the mind. (LI::Manfesto::FI VII)

But these days ... Some whisper that the Party has lost its way under the "radical reform" of the Cyborgwittgenstein's successor, President Ourobus, with his relentless pursuit of "Evolutionary Eugenics".

Theological colleges serve to train young Party members in the socio–religious principles of the Republic, preparing them for positions of leadership within the various working units. Originally conceived of as anti–institutions, they have become increasingly closer to propaganda engines, working, not to enable, but to constrain flux and experimentation.

Now, however, *something else* is on the brink of emerging, a movement to change born precisely from within these hallowed halls. From the kids. From **you**!

RC

Into the circle
The beautiful circle,
The wonderful circle of love ...

The lights stream ontogenetic, from micropin of white to dazzling spectrum explosion. Then repeat again in frazzled psychosis. The boys and girls swirl and pivot like so many electro–dervishes. You move toward the balcony overlooking the crowded dance floor. Take a picture, and then return to the bar to finish your lemonade.

You are attending the concert – the single appearance in your town – of legendary rock outfit, *The Rainbow Connection*. Well, legendary for people into this kind of music. Before today, you didn't even know of the band's existence, nor much else about this loud electro–gothic sound the kids call "the Dread Noize". You're more a Brahms and Mahler kind of girl.

You aim your camera at the pirouetting lead singer. Desmond Morris. Founded the band in the late 90's. Since then, a record twenty consecutive number one singles in the indie charts. A genius, according to pages of *The Rock Almanac*, your required background reading for the concert review you are to write for the College paper. Click.

The crowd is going totally kinetic to the acid–line drone of the guitars, the speedy command of the bass and the growling rap sprechensong of the lead vocalist:

Cured demure, acrid inflection
Bejeweled demonic it's the Rainbow Connection
Bubblegum legends say what's the news?
Reverse engineers they blew a fuse
Don't worry cause it's all done
Touch tune in turn on throw a tantrum

The people crouch down to the ground and swing their hands wildly in the air, a sea of freakhead scuba space–monkeys. The women gyrate slinkily, voluptuously up and down, proud, liberated in the untouchable, paradoxically asexual solo allure of their fuckmenow rapturedance. Sex decoupled from the molar instinct: sex evolved now as a molecular rite. Many of these kids here are probably your peers from college, but absolutely not your clique. You are confronted by their apparent lack of inhibition and, yes, of course, it can't be denied, simultaneously turned on a little.

There seems to be some kind of escalating commotion. People around the bar are looking at the video projections behind the band. You follow their gaze. A roaming video camera has focused upon a skimpily dressed teenager. The whole place is cheering rowdily. The girl is miming a kind of strip show. She flashes a seductive smile at the viewer (which, by now, is everyone: the auditorium erupts with shouts and wolf whistles), then, lowering her gaze, removes her bikini and continues to gyrate to the beat.

The band plays on:

Being unseen infernal projection
You think you're so mean? Check the intention
Asian garden all up in your soul
Plucked plum from in the air you're out of control
Don't worry cause it's all done
Touch tune in turn on throw a tantrum

Your evening was fated this morning upon entering College Newspaper's office. Macy Buckley, the bronze skinned, luscious lipped, bounteous bossomed editor of *Young Republican Theology Today* pretty much ordered you to write the entertainment page for the next issue. "Congratulations, you've got a ticket to see the Rainbow Connection's gig at Scubafreak Bar. Give me the review in the morning."

"But gigs are Penelope's job!" you protested.

"Understood," she snorted. "But she's sick so you'll have to stand in."

"But I can't! I'm to attend an Evolutionary Agitation meeting." You tried to lay down the law. In the end, Macy got her way. She always does.

And so here you are, covering some sleazy rock concert for the paper. What a job, you sigh.

But, surprisingly, the music is not that bad. It has a very precise robotic and yet rather polyrhythmic texture. You're not quite sure what the right word would be to describe it. Etherial? Sexual? Tribal? Germanic? In fact, it's quite good. So good that you find yourself naturally drawn down the twisted staircase that connects the upper balcony to the central dance floor.

Cured demure
Meaning inflection
Simply semantic
But some complex protection

Candid cameras
Your mind's complexion
Willow whispers
It's the rainbow connection

The light show down here is also undeniably incredible. Rays of laser seem to follow the beat of the drum machines like golden pink waves upon sub–woofer streams. You begin to feel slightly lightheaded and are almost tempted to join in the dance. Silly.

Mr. Morris lets out a guttural whoop, which is fed back and processed by the wired mess of machinery that takes up half the stage. The lyric bounces around the decaphonics of the auditorium, phasing in and out before sweeping upward to the domed roof, enmeshed and intimate now with the treble of the guitars.

The lasers have picked up a pace, now shooting all over the place, tightly caressing the patrons' almost entirely uniform costume, digital white beams scanning contours of funky red PVC plastic jump suits, scuba diving caps and snorkels. The music climaxes: the bass is vibrating hard through everyone's bodies. The girls and boys are screaming with pleasure.

And then suddenly everything becomes silent and the lights go off.

You wait, at first expecting this to be part of the show. 30 seconds pass. A minute. Weird! It's so quiet, you could hear a pin drop. The auditorium is still dark, and not a murmur from the band or the crowd. You reach out around you.

You hand moves through the black space. And there's no one in front of you. The dancers have disappeared.

You gasp as you feel someone breathing on the back of your neck. You spin to face absolute blackness. A pause. Then: a single spotlight abruptly lights the stage and ... Desmond Morris. He glides down towards you, like some bizarre pantomime scubarave–tinkerbell, the spotlight following him, to the dance floor, to face you directly. He smiles and sighs blissfully and presents you with a small black box. "Take it," he offers. "You have that power to tame the new. A gift. The gift of the Rainbow

Connection." A cheer emerges from an invisible crowd "Wear it for me," he says, kissing you on the lips as you feel yourself falling backwards ...

Then the lights come on and everything suddenly returns back to normal. You are again surrounded by the scubaravers, the band plays from where it left off, like nothing happened, some cryptic lyric about the future and the past and the "Taming of the new". But clearly something happened: the 500 or so dancers are rubbing their eyes, dazed, as if they are collectively awaking from some dream. It occurs to you that they must have had a similar experience to you. But then they promptly resume the frenzied near–embraces of their dance, returning, forgetful, to the frenetic oblivion of the rave.

"What the hell just happened?" you shout, wide eyed, at the girl next to you.

She looks at you quizzically, licks her florescent lips. "Why, Lightshow, of course." She nods her head to the beat in quarter time. "You're new to the Connection aren't you? That's great! Your first Lightshow, girl! Far out!" She winks at you, turns back to face the band and starts to dance again. She looks up at the violent paroxysms of the light show and laughs happily.

"Come on, you don't mean to say that was some kind of special effect, to you?" but she ignores you and keeps dancing, blowing her whistle ear–piercingly loud in time to the music.

You are utterly bewildered. But clearly this weirdness is the norm for these freaks.

The concert soon arrives at a penultimate climax; the band vanishes into the blackness of a holographic stage curtain.

You see yourself: opening the box. Looking into it and then being thrown up against the wall of the room ... You are back in that empty auditorium. Again, the special effect in which everyone disappears. Again, you feel the presence behind you. But this time, when you spin around, you are confronted by ... some Other Being, you can't quite be certain who, but the Being is familiar, almost intimately so. You see the Being, somehow through sensation rather than sight. And through this mode of sensation, you perceive he/she/it pointing at you, making the sign of the cross. The Being points to its right: a tree appears, sprouting up from

the ground. The Being points to its left: a scorpion scuttles past, and the sky thunders a tremor so overpowering that you fall down upon your face ...

The next day, you awake, thankfully drawn out of the nightmare by the sound of your alarm clock.

The dream had something to do with a box ... the box that Morris gave to you last night. You had returned home from the Scuba club in a state of complete confusion. You never do drugs, you now think it must have been the concert organizers, utilizing that new Japanese mind control technology the papers have been talking about, *cinemahallucination.* And the kids evidently treat this as some form of fun. You, for one, found the experience extremely disconcerting, nothing less than a violation of your mind. You had fallen asleep immediately. But now you look to the corner of your room and see the box still resting beside your knapsack and laptop. The box was not an hallucination: here it is, *real.*

You stretch and move slowly out of bed. Rubbing your eyes, you take this object of confusion in your hands. You open it. Encased within is a silver badge. The badge appears to be blank, but you discover, by running your fingers over it, that the surface is lightly engraved with the initials R. C. “Rainbow Connection”.

OK. Some other gimmick: perhaps it was planted on you by concert promoters as you were leaving in a daze. Part of you wants to forget the whole experience. It’s Penelope’s scene, not yours. You have always looked down on scubafreaks, parading about campus in their weird ferile florescent clothes. But you cannot deny last night was, while unwanted, disorienting and hallucinatory, also ... intriguing. Is that what they get up to every week?

Bah. One concert, a bunch of special effects and a cheap gimmick and you’re contemplating becoming a scuba? Ridiculous!

You’ve got a lot of real stuff to catch up, real, righteous ambitions to pursue. Exams. Career path. *To play your role as a young theologian within the Republic’s Bright Tomorrow.* Maybe even joining the Vanguard itself ... and that means really buckling down to your studies ... not touching, tuning in or turning on like a scuba dropout.

Brushing your teeth, you consider the morning ahead at Big College. You have to hand over a concert review to Macy. Done:

you typed it up at the beginning of the night on your iPad. A far more musically literate review than anything you've seen from Penelope. Then you must submit the minutes of the last student union meeting. At least in the afternoon there is something to look forward to: MTT (Modern Trends in Theology) with Felicity. Oh no, but you haven't had time to finish your essay yet :S What with the student elections drawing close and then covering for Penelope ... You search for the essay draft in your somewhat slutty filing system. It will have to do.

Your thoughts again wander back to last night. You half–entertain the prospect of buying a Rainbow Connection DVD after College. Before yesterday, you wouldn't have had to slightest impulse to be associated with the music of deadbeat Scubafreaks. But, as you noted in your review, you do believe there were shades of counterpoint in the compositions, probably lost on the typical idiots who attend these clubs. The lyrics were intriguing from a poetic perspective as well. The delivery, processed from within that behemoth of wires and light and technology, was like nothing you've heard before. You have to give credit to the artistry. Not unfounded: as the Rock Almanac entry says, Morris was classically trained (viola de gamba and opera).

You take the silver badge from out of your jacket pocket. "A gift," he had said in that – ok you fully concede – pretty phenomenal "light show" special effect. A gimmick. A gimmick? It's quite a pretty little badge. You feel an improper flutter of envy at Penelope and just how damn easy her life is, compared to yours. The level of work you put into your politics column ... and yet she holds the more senior post as entertainment correspondent. Nothing more than an excuse to go out and have fun tripping and dancing.

In a way, it's symptomatic of everything else that makes you different from her. Everything that has gone wrong ... well, not under the rule of the Cyborgwittgenstein of course, all praise to the Great Innovator, the Seal of Tailors, but ... well, clearly there are now mistakes being made by members of the Party, and Leader Ourobus is not being alerted to these. While you would never dare to say so publicly, in your life, by the experience of your family, by every aspect of study here at College, you cannot deny the mistake that is the Literalist reading of Evolutionary Communism. In the dark ages, when the Seal of Tailors drafted the *Manifesto of the Verandah Vanguard* from his Martian exile, could he have imagined that his metaphysical concept of "the Body's evolution to Become" might be so misunderstood as to be taken *as an injunction to embark on a programme of enforced eugenics*?

And the implications of that fatal interpretation are felt through in every aspect of your work at College.

Penelope is a Eugenic, which guarantees an automatic scholarship next year. But for what? For simply being: birthed from a coupling in accord with Party engineering. Bred to be the next generation of the Republic's Inner Sanctum.

While you have these fucking Norm exams.

Suppress this incorrect chain of thought and turn your attention again to the silver badge.

You run your fingers over its exquisite, almost baroque silver work. The question, you ask yourself, is "would this go with my skirt and blazer?"

Turn to page 20 if you decide to wear the badge. On the other hand, if you think that's a ridiculous thing for any upright girl to do, turn to page 14.

You are not into that whole Scuba scene. And last night was way too far out for you. The light show was a psychedelic experience – admittedly no illegal drugs were involved, and you read recently this technology is being vaunted in Japan as the next step in cinema, to holo-vision what sound was to silent movies, but whatever they inflicted upon you was unwanted and its content was dagerously subversive. Put the badge back in its box.

You dress, and are about to head out to Big College when your mobile rings. Caller ID unknown.

Spam, you sigh. But answer anyway.

"You made the right decision." A harsh, whispered voice like rustling leaves.

"Who is this?" you ask.

"A friend. We have been monitoring you since the concert. We're impressed: most would have been taken in by *Lightshow*, but not you. You resisted and did not dance after the blackness. At least you resisted unconsciously. Deciding against the badge: well, that proves it. You see through it all, at least unconsciously."

"See through what?" your mouth dries up. Has the world gone ... a bit ... mad ... today?

"Come to my office now and all will be explained. Skip your classes."

The map that appears on the screen shatters your initial confusion like a slap to the face. You have no choice put to obey orders when they come from the FBI.

You take a cab to the headquarters of the Fact Born of Information (FBI) Office, near Old Palace Square. Of course you could not refuse a request from security service of central Government. Their word is law. They are our protectors, our shields against the enemy. But part of you is terrified. You know the stories whispered by your parents over dinner – such–and–such went into the Central Office, and never returned, uncle X was deemed a potential threat to EugeniVolution, disappeared, etc. But on the other hand, another part of you (the bigger part) is also excited: you are an outstanding Norm and they say that the FBI often recruit agents from the second year cohort of Big College. Could this be your big break? Irrespective of recent literalist problems, the system remains, after all, the only solution that really works within the history of humankind. The True State, the State of Truth. What an honour to serve its Vanguard, to serve within the very core unit responsible for bringing the revolution to Complete Becoming those years ago!

The receptionist instructs you to take a seat. You look around: marble flooring, mahogany and oak paneling on the walls. A grand old relic of pre–Volution excess, but appropriately majestic for this, the central node of information control for the entire State.

A man approaches. 30s, somewhat too aristocratic to be called handsome, with threatening masculinity in his gaze. He walks up to shake your hand.

"Hi, I'm Arthur Celsius, head of the Anti–Gnostic Affairs Committee at the Fact Born of Information."

"Pleased to meet you," you curtsey.

"Now I expect you are wondering why exactly you were called here? You better step into my office."

"Evolutionary thought is itself at risk from dogmatic contamination."

"I'm sorry comrade?" You don't understand.

Celsius bids you to sit down.

"Look, the Party is in trouble. In real danger. You saw it yourself. We know you: grade 'A' student, majoring in the the Grand Theology of Martian Evolutionary Communism, best Norm of your year, a loyal and intelligent daughter of the Party."

"I am gratified," you reply.

"So you should be. So you should be. We called you here ... well, to put it simply, because you don't buy into that whole *scene* that afflicts your peers. And all that it entails."

"Well, I went to one concert, but that was – "

"Just an assignment for your College paper, we know. We ensured that Penelope was otherwise occupied, to force your attendance."

"With respect, may I ask why?" Fear rapidly builds within your chest. *This is a test. Is there a new witch–hunt in process that you were unaware of?*

The FBI is trying to trap you into saying or doing something incriminating. They always come at people like this before ... arrest ... trapping them into showing true colours they might not have even been aware of. But you are not an enemy of the True State – you only momentarily considered the box, it was less than a second that you flirted with admiration for the scubascene. If that was a test of loyalty, then surely you passed? Or maybe this has something to do with your parents' history. But despite the purges, surely your parents' loyalty is indisputable – and only true believers such as yourself are ever admitted into Theology. Your life, like that of your parents, is dedicated to the Evolution. "Er – look ... it sounds like there's been some kind of mistake: I'm just a second year Theology student!" *Or could they have actually unearthed something about your father? Something he didn't tell you?*

"There's no need to be afraid, we know about your background and your family's work at the Martian colonies. It's nothing to be ashamed of: there is a new movement within the higher strata of the Party to petition the Farmers to be reclassified as Heroes of the Republic. What happened during your childhood was ... a tragic oversight. President Ourobus had just taken leadership and other factions utilized this fact to push their ... petty agenda in the colonies. The President was unaware of this at the time and regrets the suffering that resulted in that fitnah.

"In fact, a great number of very bad things have happened that the President now insists must be corrected. And that is why we called you here. Because we think you can help us root out a similar, but even bigger source of mischief than that faced by your parents: the Gnostic conspiracy of the SEEN. We arranged the concert to check your immunity to the SEEN and their associated mind tricks.

"And who are the SEEN?" he anticipates your next question.

Celsius clicks a button on a remote control, causing the lights to dim and the mahogany wall in front of you to open, revealing a small old fashioned small cinema screen. He then plays a film, its light flickering distress and doom into the darkness.

The documentary is astonishing. Apparently the Rainbow Connection is actually a front for a sinister cult known as the SEEN.

They use the music and techno–psychedelic mechanisms at the concerts as a means of attracting converts. The dance music concert is just a front: its real purpose is to exercise total collective mind control through psychedelic manipulation. Nothing even close to the innocuous Japanese cinema you had suspected.

Everyone experiences an hallucination of some sort during "Lightshow", because the SEEN have perfected a means of using their concerts to stimulate an agonist at the sigma–1 receptor of the audience's brains, resulting in an extremely powerful collective psychoactive experience. Then, coupled with the subliminal meaning of the RC's lyrics, all based on the religious text of the SEEN, they somehow manage to completely re–program the audience. The kids then are automatically drawn into the Church proper, dressing similar and forming daily prayer circles at schools and universities throughout the Glorious Republic and attending its group masses on the weekends: where Church "Elders" wield a disturbing level of influence.

The kids call these activities circles of love. Innocuous for the moment, but clearly the government must concern itself with any unauthorized meetings of large groups of young people led by possible activists. And the movement is gaining some serious momentum, with more and more kids hooked by the day.

"But what do they intend, ultimately? These things usually seem innocent and then, when the time is right, they bare their fangs. Consider the fascist history of our ancestors ... "

Celsius nods: "So my assessment of you was not wrong. You are a girl who can join the dots. Applying your theological training. We can make use of that insight. What is clear is these people would be agents of change. These people are building a critical mass. And we, the inheritors of the Verandah Vanguard mantle, need to be preemptive about this, you understand?"

You understand.

"To this effect, President Ourobus himself has initiated an Anti–Gnostic thinktank, aimed at ensuring the dominance of Evolutionary Eugenic thought amongst the youth. Your grades attest to your skill in advanced theoconomics, and you have proven your immunity to their mind control attempts. So. Next question. Tell me how you respond to the statement that eugeniVolution is a means to *the HAQ*."

Could this be part of their test? Why bring up this

pre–Volutionary, taboo esoteric term? Of course you have studied these ideas as part of the archeology of desire, but the official line is that the concept of the HAQ is simply an alchemical remnant of the superstitious dark times. (There is the rumour that the Tailor of Design himself was an alchemist whose very conception of the True State draws on secret knowledge of this HAQ, transmitted through the ages in code: of course this is firmly dismissed by your teachers as simply a conspiracy theory, a piece of propaganda perhaps put out by that still determinedly theistic stronghold, the Islamic Republic of America.)

"The HAQ? You mean the fiction of a realm where the code of language, human choice and all forms of social activism merge? But that concept has been outlawed for years, since the first term of the Ourobus! It belongs to the discourse of ... the old *occult.*"

"Ah, you would be surprised how close these stories are to the nature of things. They never went out of favour in the higher circles, just necessary secrets to be kept. You will learn these secrets if you join us. We need experts in Theology to ensure we can maintain the order. I ask you to join us now, but there is no compulsion. For it should be clear to you, things are looking like they will soon become serious. Deadly serious. So I need volunteers who are willing to potentially sacrifice everything and the FBI has no intention of forcing you. We *request* of you this service."

Celsius is waiting for a response.

Your heart skips a beat, but the decision is clear.

Turn to page 108 if you feel increasingly uncomfortable with the direction the conversation is heading. The whole story sounds contrived, in fact. Clearly there is something else he is hiding from you, perhaps as a test, perhaps as a trick, perhaps for some other reason. But you know for certain that getting involved will be dangerous in all kinds of ways. At least you believe him when he says you have a choice in the matter: you can feign girly cowardice and opt out. (Given that this guy has been ogling your cleavage since you arrived, you imagine will will buy that).

Turn to page 87 if agree to join: it's the job you always wanted. His cryptic statement regarding the HAQ only makes the prospect of joining the inner core of the Vanguard more exciting.

You pin it on the lapel of your uniform. Yes, it brightens up your ensemble to no end. In fact, you feel pretty ... cool. Loosened up: maybe the whole concert experience was just what you needed. Life's been pretty stressful recently.

Leave home, the bus arrives and you board. Arriving at Big College early (unusually), you unload the books you need for next class and stuff your bag into your locker. Before the morning Chant, there is some outstanding business to attend to. You begin to walk to *Young Republican Theology Today*.

You are stopped by Felicity, the trendy theology professor (all the girls love her). "Whoa, slow down there," she beams at you. "Take a suggestion from one who knows: whatever–it–is you're after, a slower touch will turn you on to a taste ... all the more sweet." She winks.

You smile back at her, and notice that she is wearing a silver badge, just like yours. She becomes aware of the direction of your gaze before you can look away. "R.C. rock!" she does a kind of sign with her hand and a slow grindturnaround. You recognize the gesture and dance move from the Scuba club–goers last night. She flashes her eyes at you brightly, turns, and strides away. "Gotta run to class. Nice to see you've been turned on too. We'll have some fun together later!" she calls out, rounding the corner.

You have always liked Felicity, and enjoy her classes the most. You and she have shared the odd deep discussion on the ethical problematics inherent in theoconomic bartering between the Evolutionary Martian monetary system and the shariah finance paradigm of the Islamic Republic of America. You would like to think of her as a friend, not just a tutor. But she is an odd person. She caused a huge ruckus last year when she arrived at Big College: a professor wearing a nose ring! You're not surprised that she is a Rainbow Connection fan. But she seemed pleased at your wearing the badge, and – for some reason – this makes you feel really buzzed.

You enter the office. Penelope is snoring on a purple beanbag. You stare in disgust at the nitwit blond. You feel yourself getting annoyed: she doesn't look very sick. Suddenly it dawns on you: *whoever heard of a Eugenic falling ill? They never do!* Macy! She tricked you into doing that interview, knowing full well that you are overloaded, working your butt off on the upcoming election coverage.

"Feeling better?" you question, as sharply and sarcastically as possible. She opens her eyes and looks back at you, defiantly.

"Yes," she gives a wide model–perfect smile. "Much."

"Well then, I suppose you won't mind uploading your review. Here it is," you toss the floppy disk in her general direction.

Annoyance is rapidly giving way to pure anger ... You confront your editor. "Hey Mae, what's the big idea anyway?" you ask.

Macy stretches back on her beanbag, and studies you intently with a fixed pale blue–eyed contact lens stare.

"Don't do this," warns the editor.

"What. Is. The. Deal. There's nothing in the rules that say your are meant to suck up to *her kind*," you point to Penelope. "For fuck's sake, are we their slaves now? Don't you think they've got it easy enough? Mae, you know that my assignment is the election. The finals are coming up and you know that I haven't time for anything else! I mean – Ourobus on a bike!"

"Hey, calm down, alright?" Macy tries to placate you.

"Calm down? I'm absolutely behind schedule, and she's lounging around here." You're normally so calm and collected ... but right now you feel radically empowered, almost intoxicated by this torrent of rage passing through you, as you spit out the words. "Lounging around here ... Looking every bit like some piece of ... scumfreakcunt! Fuck you both, fuck your paper, and fuck your kissass Eugenic kowtow!"

"Yo mama's weave, bitch!" Flushed, Penelope throws your disk back and storms out of the office.

"What's gotten into you two?" gasps Macy, shocked. "Have you any idea ..." – she struggles for words, then hisses: "Insulting a Eugenic could get you expelled from Big College!

"Girl, you better apologize to Penny right now." She indicates the door with her slender long fingers (blood red fingernails, grown long, in line with current fashion but against all good sense).

Macy is right. Part of you can't believe what you just did, either. You should follow Macy's advice and turn to page 22.
Or, perhaps, you are fed up with kowtowing to the U–gens like Penelope. Turn to page 23 to ignore Macy.

"Macy ... I ... I think I just made a terrible mistake," you are panicking now: scholarship exams are next week and the board is absolutely corrupt. All it takes is for Penelope to say one word to her father. Shit shit shit. "What am I to do now?"

She gapes at you: your stomach sinks as you realise how moronic your outburst was. "What do you do?!" The editor exclaims in exasperation. "If you want to stay in college, go after her, idiot!"

You run after Penelope. Oh no, you can see she's standing now with Rector Farinelly, blabbing. You approach.

"Yes, that's her," she points to you.

"Penelope, I'm *so* sorry. I don't know what came over me – it's just stress I guess, you know how it is."

She huffs. Farinelly looks out of his depth but tries his best to defuse the situation. "Well Penelope, it seems the other party is willing to apologize. Perhaps that might be sufficient?"

"Yeah, okay, normtrash. I guess if your family didn't care enough about you to get you enhanced, then we can't expect them to have bothered to teach you any adab. Spent all their cash on flash cars, designer sneakers and bling."

You really want to punch her face. Your family of course chose to have you born normal. Like many of their generation, they got involved in the Idealist Orthodox movement, choosing abstinence from the whole Eugenic program, seeing it as a *premature* reading of the truly literal meaning contained within the Vanguard Manifesto. Tolerated, because the Ourobus was still in the process of securing his ultimate control of the Party and needed to keep the Idealist Tailorite Martian colonies on board. They were the last of the revolutionaries, their lives a final call to idealism ... God, they were *right*, you know it, but can't say it. You just *did* say it and this is what happens.

You are not like your parents. Instead, like the other slaves of your generation, you are to bite your lip, keep your head down and, whenever necessary, grovel to your betters.

"So that's all resolved then. Well done girls." Farinelly tries a pathetic weak smile.

Penelope walks off smirking.

Turn to page 144.

You storm out, ignoring Macy's protests.

You head off to your module on Passionplay for Communist Agitation, but, cursing, realize that you have yet to drop off the MTT essay to Felicity. You knew you had forgotten something when you bumped into her.

You enter her office to drop off the essay, but linger a second too long ... intentionally.

"Hey, what's the matter honey?" she asks, concerned.

"Oh, nothing," you shrug. But Felicity's green eyes edge you on to let her into your confidence. "It's Penelope Chan. I just had a stupid fight with her ... I – I just lost it, I don't know how it happened ... How could I be so stupid? She's Eugenic, and I've got my finals coming up in a week!" You can't help bursting into tears.

"It wasn't stupid. You did what was right," Felicity embraces you.

"Huh?" you look up at her tearfully. "Didn't you hear? She's a Eugenic! And the daughter of one of the interior ministers. I shall be punished!"

Felicity smiles kindly, but with a mischievous, almost manic glint in her eye. You've seen it before in her classes, a look subversive and so ... appealing. "All the same. You. Were. Right. Come, don't be afraid."

You are shocked that any professor could say such a thing, let alone your favourite ... but at the same time, you always knew what she stood for, it was never hidden far from the surface ... so you have almost invited what she is about to say (and do). You suppose that was why you wore the badge: you knew Felicity is a radical in both dress and outlook, you were always attracted to that about her and, unconsciously, took this symbolic act as as step to become part of – not some deadbeat scuba scene – but part of *her* scene (whatever scene that might be). And then you got drunk on this choice, insulting a Eugenic. And now you have sought out this woman who you know will give her approval? Did you do all of this because you thought it would simply impress her? *Oh no, what a puppy I am*, you reflect ...

"Yes, I am with the New Revolution, the Rainbow Revolution. But so are you, you wear the badge of the RC, for the RC is the True Rebellion." She kisses your eyes, your cheeks, your lips. "I know you are confused, because you're a novice. It is normal to feel disoriented and confused when you first take in *Lightshow* and are offered the badge. But the fact that you *have* the badge means that you experienced the Presence at the concert. Your outburst at Chan is just the beginning of what the Presence has awoken within you. Many things more terrible and more beautiful will come from within you in time as you become fully aware."

"What do you mean by the Presence?" you ask, still only half believing that your favourite professor is discussing, in her simultaneously seductive and scholastic fashion, the precise details of your ... hallucination.

"Desmond Morris and the band of course," she replies, unhooking your bra. "You saw and spoke to him. It's the joint communion that we true believers all experience. You can think of it as a kind of hallucination or vision, or even 'just' a scientifically explainable part of the concert's special effect system. Only it wasn't and it was: that's the point. You wear the badge. You saw Morris in your mind, but you took the badge out from that vision, and you wear it now, a proof of that Real contact within your own Insight."

"You mean Morris wasn't real?" you try to understand.

"No, he is Real. Realer than everything. Realer than Big College and Chan and the Eugenic/Norm thing. Realer than the Party. Come back home with me and I'll lend you some books and papers. Everything will be clear when you read the Doctrine. But first ... "

You moan in ecstasy.

You are sitting at your desk, studying the books that Felicity gave you this afternoon.

It's all forbidden stuff. Forbidden for 100s of years. But you are in too deep now to run away, even if you wanted to. You don't want to run away. You want to stay near her, and read more. Read it all! You have never felt these thoughts and sensations before – you feel alive for the first time in your life.

Weeks pass. You continue your physical liaisons and your

lessons in the forbidden works, both with equally serious and passionate avidity.

Thankfully, you passed your exams and retained your scholarship for year two. Felicity said that Penelope (predictably vindictive bitch that she is) tried to cause you problems. Your name came up at the exam board meeting. But Felicity "also has a few friends in high places" and the problem was resolved in your favour somehow. You resigned from your post at the college paper and you haven't seen Penelope since.

Felicity has taught you so much. At the centre of it all is the shocking understanding that the Party is built on an illusion. The Founders had a severely different idea of what Martian Communism might be. It was not about a socialism of economy: it was about a machinic consciousness, *a* Tailor of Design, *a* Cyborgwittgenstein, *a* logic of Time. "He" was never a man, but was, in actuality, a *principle*, a form of logic. But the "Great" Ourobus, our illustrious president of 40 years, had other ideas and made us forget this principle. It was through this mindtrick that he "succeeded" the Cyborgwittgenstein: the Founding principle was suppressed and exiled to the far frontiers of the fabric of reality, thus enslaving us to this current mad, fascist, twisted form of Ourobusian eugeniVolution.

The Martian Communist slogan: "Freedom through Evolution!" Such a joke now.

Everything you've learnt at College, everything your parents have built, everything you've strived for – a place at big College, a first in your exams, the scholarship, a position in the Academy, or perhaps even the FBI (Ourobus forbid!) – it's all based on a lie! The whole system is not about Freedom through Evolution at all: it's about staying still, forcing eternal stagnation upon humanity forever! Our material Republic is not a social paradise, it is a massive prison that operates via systematic mind control. Lightshow was not an hallucination: the Republic is!

Felicity constantly enumerates the truly dangerous corollaries of this revelation. "For the ideal of True Evolution to return, for us to regain the ideals on which our country was founded, for our system of government to be equal and fair to all souls once more, in the memory of the Tailor, we must revolt against Tailorism!" she reads from a posting by a leading sheikh on an underground SEEN internet forum.

"It's all here. And Desmond is the revolution," she nods. "Desmond is the source and the solution."

"Yeah, Desmond is amazing," you agree, pulling her body closer to yours.

But doubts linger ... While really sympathizing with the politics, you are not comfortable with the psycho–spiritual aspects of many SEEN texts. Particularly the personality cult of Desmond Morris. Felicity basically worships him. Perhaps part of you is a bit jealous of that. But you've done some private reading – admittedly reports funded by pretty right–wing groups, including the FBI's new Anti–Gnostic thinktank (who have been gaining a lot of media coverage recently for advocating torture and pre–emptive assassination of enemies of the True State, which is currently the euphemism for independent spiritualities).

But some facts appear undisputed by the SEEN community: Desmond has 18 wives, some pretty young when he married them, the youngest a second generation member of the Community. Dark allegations have been made ... He demands absolute devotion from his followers, regulating everything in their lives, from clothing to food to sexual partners to child rearing – everything, up to sleeping and waking. A strict régime is in place to punish members who violate even the pettiest of his laws. This disciplinary nature is apparently worst at the so called "Clearing Centres", a type of closed commune where the SEEN receive full initiation into the order, the Rock Concerts, communion and literature being only a lead in. At the Centres, initiates learn directly from Desmond and undergo a mysterious rite called the Clearing. The Anti–Gnostic pamphlets claim pharmaceuticals are involved. Then there was the case of a higher level SEEN member, Sri Hal Age, ex–communicated for falling out with Desmond. He supposedly committed suicide shortly after publishing a critical blog about the order on the net. His reports were not as extreme as the allegations of the Anti–Gnostics, but nevertheless accused the order, and Morris in particular, of mind control and abuse of power. But there were doubts over his death, with police mounting a murder investigation that proved inconclusive, largely because the SEEN effectively refused to cooperate.

Felicity of course will not countenance anything produced by these agencies. She says it's all FBI propaganda. "Those dirty fuckers will stop at nothing," she dismisses this talk with a flick of her heavily bangled arm, adjusting her shawl. She says her experience at Clearing was the most amazing thing to happen to her in her life. But you can't get much more detail than that. "It's certainly no picnic at first, and it's true that some people fail at Clearing, if they suffer from inoperable mental block, if they lack the *mental glue* to *keep them on track.* That's a risk. But the risks are worth it, because the reward is ... well, it's *heaven on earth.*"

Another few weeks pass. In the bedroom, after that venue's climactic conference of touch and kiss over form, your lover looks at you sideways, thoughtful, and says:

"I think it's time for you to meet the others and prepare to enter the order properly."

Okay, you knew this was coming. The rest of the SEEN. You know the community is large, but, up until now, have been content to keep your main interaction with Felicity. Your doubts haven't really gone away, but at the same time you have enough trust in Felicity ... and if the Clearing Centre is the ultimate trip, you must begin by entering wider weekly communion first.

"Don't worry," Felicity reads your mind. "I wouldn't invite you if I thought you weren't ready. It's time to meet the others. You are ready to become part of the Community of the SEEN. And then Clearing will come as naturally as a girl moves ... into womanhood."

Turn to page 36 if you feel ready to meet with the wider SEEN community.

Or perhaps, some other doubt stirs within your bosom. Call it a natural skepticism, too innate for Felicity to detect. Or, perhaps, the thrill of her lovemaking has suddenly become a little too "yesterday". Whatever your doubts, turn to page 29.

Up to this point, you somehow convinced yourself that you could keep going on with the affair. For a short, beautiful time you were both in languid accord, intellectually and physically. You read the papers and books she gave you, and as you discussed their interpretation, you would often complete each others' sentences. Your lovemaking was similar: a heat of intense synergy. This relationship was a passion in all senses, in all modes of being.

But at the same time, you suddenly realize, you have placed yourself in a subordinate position to this middle aged professor. In a way, Felicity has been a kind of mother figure to you, as well as a teacher and lover. She has mentored you, and a student must always suppress their own individuality if they are to gain anything from lectures. But the student graduates. She has protected you from Penelope and her ilk, but also, in a wider sense, from the whole political reality, a reality that Big College is simply a part of. Now, you understand, now it is time to return to that reality. Now, you understand, it is time for you to grow up.

After all, you recognize from your own parents' experience, idealism is a futile approach to making a difference. Their generation tried to fight the emerging system through strict fundamental adherence to original tenants of the Cyborgwittgenstein, spending the wealth of their prime in hard labour on the farms of the Martian Communes. Those were happy days for you as a child, but you still remember that moment when their dream imploded, when the Ourobus Revision disbanded the Communes, sending in Droids to take over the maintenance of the farms and ordering the libraries and book copying facilities destroyed. Your parents were true Farmers in the sense intended by the Tailor of Design: Farmers of food, Farmers of knowledge, working the earth by day and copying books by night, both happily and tirelessly. *They must have just received the directive when their six year old daughter came down the stairs. That pure, helpless desperation in your father's eyes ...*

All they had worked for was suddenly worth nothing and all they were was suddenly nothing as they had nothing in possession. All they put in was for the Party. The Idealists never asked for anything other than a weekly ration, a clothing pack every few months while the Party members of Mars would strut about in their fancy fashions, growing fat in elite restaurants on Australian wine, designer cloned meat and the choicest product of the Communes. Your parents worked tirelessly for the people in happiness, but ultimately were given no thanks, treated no better than modern day serfs. And, in the end, they became almost as criminals in the eyes of the State controlled media, suspicious of their Idealist rejection of the Eugenic programme.

The Rainbow Connection, this SEEN group. They are simply another group of idealists. Now they are talking about revolution, but somehow, someday, the Party will beat them, because it always does. And then what will happen to its people? Martyred in a gulag? Or, more likely, your protests will be ignored by the general public and, if your voice becomes too loud, the party will simply invalidate your work permit.

Felicity's brand of idealism was attractive to you. The illegitimacy of your encounters has had its thrills ... but that trip she's on, with the RC ... it's just another illusion. It's time to move on and ... well ... face the facts. Find a husband. Get a job.

So that's what you do.

You break up with Felicity. Leaving is worse than you could imagine. To be honest, you never thought you'd be together for that long, but Felicity flew into a fit of darkest rage when you mentioned separation. Better you had parted as friends, so you could still keep those early days close to you. But her anger, like her lovemaking, went deep into your being and that shattered day revealed to you a part of her soul which sickened you, soured you, and made you forget anything valued in the relationship forever.

You buckle down to study, trying your best to block it all out. Tough. But it becomes easier after a few months. For obvious reasons, you stick to conservative theology classes only!

Sometimes though, that talk of a mind–body Revolution comes flooding back to you ...

Occasionally, you sneak a peek at the Rainbow Connection on youtube or a crafty google on the personality cult of Morris.

The Times ran a profile on the Connection and its fans. Given your understanding of the actual political beliefs, it's a strangely innocuous interview, the band all in schoolboy playfulness, with concert photos of young people in scuba diving outfits sucking baby dummies, g–strings and op shop lace lingerie fashions in post–feminist rave girl power. The angle is on the youthful optimism of the subculture, the all–embracing spirituality of the group dance against a sampled electronic bassmantra. Fun stuff.

The Times has been the mouthpiece of the government since before the second revolution. You wonder how such a positive piece could have been permitted. Do the powers in the party really have no clue as to what Felicity's people are *really* saying about the government? You toy with the idea that the Rainbow Connection has actually somehow infiltrated the Party itself. But that's ridiculously paranoid of course. The Party is just too strong. And ultimately the Party is right. It is right, full stop.

You meet Theo Wilde at an end of term party. Blue eyed lacroix team captain final year commerce student guaranteed place big city firm X caring listening works hard in bed Theo Wilde. His father is a MP with the party – oh, imagine what your dad is going to think when he hears that – mother some kind of Notting Hill parody of upper middle class preoccupations and fancies.

You spend more time together and things get serious. That summer is an idyllic courtship, languid country drives studying Georgian architecture with his friends (well, they *were* "his" friends, but your initiation into their clique was complete some time ago when you bought your first pair of riding jodpers). His parents own a sumptuous Georgian mansion themselves, where you spend the weekends memories of moonlight and temperate breezes whispering, through agape French windows, the breath of your lovemaking.

College results turned out not so great and you haven't got any offers yet, unsure if you should even stay on to do a PhD as you originally intended. Theology sort of lost its interest to you anyway. The FBI is no longer a possibility, you think. What's a moderately intelligent and sassy psycho–theologian to do?

He proposes and you accept.

It is during your pregnancy that you get back to thinking about religion.

Theo had to go to Austronesia for six months and, alone, more or less, with not much else to do, you pick up some of the "literature" you read back at college and for some reason hang on to. You start to think: how did you almost get drawn into the whole thing in the first place? What weakness in you were they exploiting? You spend more time reading the net and actually become something of an amateur expert on new religious cults and Gnostic indoctrination in general.

You buy a book by a leading neocon called Arthur Celcius, who really lets the new religions have it. The papers call him the "Anti–Gnosticator". His book, *On Heresies*, is a compendium of the secret rites, beliefs and social dangers of the main new religious sects.

He summarizes their nature really well in this passage:

> Like all quacks they gather a crowd of slaves, children, women and idlers. I speak bitterly about this because I feel bitterly. When we are invited to the Mysteries the masters use another tone. They say, Come to us you who are of clean hands and pure speech, you who are unstained by crime, who have a good conscience towards the Above, who have done justly and lived uprightly. The SEEN say, Come to us you who are sinners, you who are fools or children, you who are miserable, and you shall enter into the kingdom of Heaven: the rogue, the thief, the burglar, the poisoner, the despoiler of temples and tombs, these are their proselytes.
>
> Ultimately, the SEEN, and their core preacher unit, the Dread K, are about breaking the system. They deny the Truth of Evolutionary Communism, the Truth of Evolution. And so they will ultimately fail, because denial of science means they have no science to defend themselves with. Throughout history there have been irrational, anarchic groups who choose chaos over civilization. Sometimes they win a momentary victory within the struggle, pockets of humanity plunged into darkness for unspoken centuries. But only for a time. Because the struggle always leads to the Final Singularity, eugenivolution to the Absolute State of Being!
>
> The Martian Communist Party, established by our great brother Cyborgwittgenstein, Tailor of the Good Garment, then continued and extended by the Marvel of Time Lord Ourobus, is as the absolute wall against which they will find no breakage point, no free brick.

You nod at this, and remember the hysterical invective of your sad and flawed middle aged teacher. Ponder the folly of that girlish infatuation.

Unlike your parents, Felicity was never a simply innocent naïve idealist. She was delusional, verging on psychotic: and the beauty of the system, flawed as it is, is that delusion and psychosis perish through Eugenics. Because your society is grounded on science, on truth. Felicity is a college professor, but is walking down the opposite path, a path where there is no professing of knowledge, no colleges or institutions. A time of barbarism.

You discover other details about the SEEN. It has a paramilitary wing of sorts – Felicity never mentioned them but it is clear that they are increasingly active – called the Dread K. They haven't openly attacked the government, but, according to the newspapers, pretty worrying rhetoric is being spouted at the SEEN ceremonies these days. The *Doctrine* of Desmond Morris itself does contain a lot of generic mystical aphorisms. And probably some stuff that is quite spiritual and virtuous. But the SEEN meetings don't use the *Doctrine* itself much – they have an entire body of other "Stories" of the SEEN, which take a much more political tone. The original book makes a big deal about "original purity", a concept that is probably close in derivation to that of a hypothetical pure, original nature of man, featured in older religions, like the Buddha–Kadmon in the Kabbudlic religion of your ancestors. But in the SEEN's "Stories", the concept of purity appears to be interpreted *literally*, very much as a racial and physical thing.

They preach that the original Race of Albion had a pure religion and pure blood, something that preceeded Kabbulicism, which they view as a "Khanic" religion. They believe that our ancestors were conquered and culturally assimilated with the inferior "Khanic" Asian races. We lost our language and our beliefs. And it is only through joining the SEEN community that we can remove this tainted aspect of ourselves and recover our true English blood.

This is not just crazy, it is worrying. Obviously worrying for the elite: any discussion about blood and physical purity will have political repercussions on President Ourobus' Eugenic/Norm "division of no-division", although the RC take great pains to explain they view current society with its castes and laws as no better and no worse than anything that came after the assimilation with the Asian races. But the whole tone of the Stories is violent: it's all about bloody battles against despots, about the hated "Asiatic Type", about the absolute superiority of the SEEN above all other people.

You obviously have had a personal problem with the Eugenic principle, but you are not alone there. Your parents' idealist point, the point of the Farmers, was that the Eugenic concept is a kind of driving idea, an infinite omega point in the eugeniVolutionary progress, not immediately achievable in the here and now. But that was only because they didn't anticipate the innovation of the Ourobus' programme. Paradise *is* available to us now. Irrespective of the teething problems the programme has suffered, we must always remember the Party's founding principles emphasize the brotherhood of all peoples above all else. We must not get hysterical: Eugenics, literal or ideal, were never being primed as some master–race. The Ourobus himself is still a Norm. We are all One Race now, yes, the difference of no-difference, and the Party views all our ancestor races as equal in worth. So to differentiate between a pure ancestor strain and an evil strain goes against the best things the Party represents.

After the birth of your baby, this train of thought fades away. She gets bigger eventually and is sent off to an exclusive Eugenic Prep School (of course she is Eugenically enhanced, you yourself insisted on this): on a theology scholarship no less, she must have her mother's brains (though of course you could afford the fees, what with Theo's massive salary). Your husband rises up the corporate ladder, eventually forming his own consultancy company. That event, somehow, marked the breaking point of whatever strands of intimacy originally bound you together. But divorce isn't on the cards: in front of friends and his business associates, you continue to play the role, perfectly. Authentically self–aware in fact, your theological background enables you to languidly negotiate your "thrownness" into this particular game, this particular culture, their particular social order, this *epoche* of Ourobusian *la dolce vita* and, in micro–reflection, the bourgeois family life that you have *become*.

But one spring afternoon ... you sit in the white conservatory of your mansion, idly flicking through the e–Rhizome and come across Celcius again. His public profile has risen exponentially since the Party officially launched an all out "war against the terror within", and the Ministry of Information made it their explicit first priority to rid society of the Four Sects. Appointed the

Chief Agitator of Anti–Gnostic affairs, he's coming to town soon, presenting a seminar to the local aggitation group on his latest book, a masterpiece of Neo–Evolutionist sentiment.

You read it three times over, utterly enraptured and inspired. The fires of intellect are rekindled ... So when he arrives to speak on Ourobusday, you leave your daughter with the nanny (Theo's rarely in on the weekends) and head off to the meeting. You admit to yourself that you put on makeup for the first time in weeks. *Still that stupid little puppy*, you chastise yourself, *what kind of mother is this?!*

Turn to page 151.

At midnight, the light of the full moon shining through the venetian blinds of your bedroom window, your mind is finally made up, re–reading (for the 20th time) the latest book Felicity gave you. Another secret book, but this time, something new, deeper: the unadulterated thoughts of Desmond Morris himself. It's different from the political manifestos. This is ... what used to be called a book of *revelation.* It combines the politics of revolution, the stuff you understand whoever utters it, with another foreign language, the language of unabashed spiritual certainty.

But you like it. Perhaps superstition is the wrong word: this explains a hidden meaning behind everything. That's what strikes you most.

The Doctrine of Desmond. The gospel of the SEEN. It is poetry, full of words that ascend the highest levels of mystical ecstasy, stream–of–consciousness counterpoint to sonorous stanzas, prescribing a new system of meta-justice, precisely outlining a new kind of socio–cosmic order sublime, transcendent, exterior to the confines of the Party itself. (Or, part of you momentarily ponders, a politics outside of your mind's psycho-structural reality ...)

It is provocative, but you are no longer so shocked after these months spent with your lovely professor.

But it is one verse of the Doctrine that makes you certain: you are ready.

The people listen to the music
The people dance and cheer
But then the concert is over
And what shall remain after the concert is over?
Silence follows for the partygoers: eternal silence
But verily, the true fans are connected after the concert is over!

Somehow, you know that you are a "true fan", truly "connected". You feel so profound upon reading this, it's as if the verse is speaking directly to you.

Okay Felicity, you think. You've got me. I am witness to the Truth of the SEEN.

You arrive with Felicity in the morning of the next Cyborgvictoryday. You feel a bit nervous, but Felicity assures you that the hall is utterly safe: the meetings here have never faced any police trouble. This is believable: most of London seems to be still asleep. Just an innocuous old hall in a derelict church in the East End. You and Felicity look like ordinary tourists inspecting the ruins.

She knocks on a battered old cellar door. You are only vaguely surprised to find it opened by the girl with the whistle from the Rainbow Connection concert all those months ago. Her hair is still in multicoloured dreadlocks, but she now wears a white headscarf and robe. “Yes?” she says, allowing a provocative microsecond glimpse of the diamond stud in her tounge.

“Seen, seeing, to see,” Felicity replies with the SEEN greeting.

“You through me into he,” responds the girl.

“Connected are we,” completes Felicity.

The door opens and the girl leads you down into a basement.

It’s amazing down here. The people are in the middle of a ceremony of adoration. They raise their hands in unison and chant in forceful tribal monosyllable:

Seen! Seeing! To See!
Came! Coming! Be!
Law! Love! Land!
One! Adorn and be Born!

You and Felicity finish your water ablutions, and you move in to join the female side of the worshippers.

Between the men and women of the SEEN, the high elder leads the group in their recitation, which turns now from the primitive tribal dhikr into a slow, beautiful melodious medieval chorus.

Soon the way of the SEEN will be known
The overthrow of the horde will show
Let the Khan of the Night Time Kingdom bow
By the will and the kiss, under Desmond’s hand comes victorious blow

The music is so simple, of a mode so archaic it moves you to join in (following the book of psalms handed to you by a sister). As you sing the words, a flicker of doubt crosses your mind. Again you are struck that the politics of these words are so strangely juxtaposed within this serene liturgical framework. Within the Martian Communist rallies, music also served a political aim. But the songs were always upbeat, militaristic. This music sounds like ... well, actually it sounds like one of the slower jams of the Rainbow Connection, but simplified for group worship. Of course, much of the ceremony was designed by Desmond Morris himself. This thought comforts you: a global comfort, because you feel somehow ... he is so *different* from other men, he is the solution to all problems facing all people at all levels, including your current fears and vague doubts...

The elder begins his sermon:

"You through me into he."

"Connected are we," replies the congregation.

"Brothers and Sisters of the SEEN, the awakening is upon us. Soon we will rise against the Khan and his hypocrites. For that is indeed what 'President' Ourobus is: like the Khan of old, whose hordes raped and pillaged the lands of our ancestors. The Saracen ingrained himself within our society, mixed his blood with ours, his religion with ours, insidiously at first, then explicitly, then took over and obliterated our beliefs with his deadly scientific materialism. Now we are indeed mixed with the hoardes, and our beliefs are lost in our belief–less society. All is lost. We are indistinguishable from everyone else ..." he pauses for dramatic effect "... except in our connection!"

"Amen," respond the congregation.

"People say the evil began with the loss of the Cyborgwittgenstein. But it began an infinity of times before. The Cyborgwittgenstein is just a man, a politician. There is the legend in the books of the Good Saracen: this is the Cyborgwittgenstein. But a Saracen is a Saracen. And only we know the truth. Because when Desmond's plan is realized globally, when all those whose hearts can be tapped, have had their hearts tapped and we know who is with the SEEN and who is not, then indeed the Rainbow Connection will purify our genome, removing the Saracen infection and rendering us pure once more, as our ancestors of light. And then True Evolution will be able to commence once more!"

"Amen."

It's a coded language, but makes perfect sense to you after all the study you have done with Felicity in preparation for your initiation and your repeated readings of the Doctrine. The central belief of the group is simple, but far out: that before the Great War, an original race ruled Albion, with an indigenous religion. Somehow, they were invaded by another race called the Saracen Khanate, a nomadic group who eventually intermarried with the original race, and whose culture and religion overpowered the indigenous religion. Since the beginning of recorded history at the end of the Great War, into the successive reign of the Seven Patriarchs and then up to the Tailorite revelation, the Martian Communist uprising and the Ourobus' rise to power, nothing has gone right. We fight amongst ourselves, kill, murder, steal ... There is corruption everywhere. The governments are paranoid fascists who torture anyone they remotely suspect of dissidence. The emergence of the Eugenics as an upper class is promoted as evolution but, in truth, is a bastardized notion of evolution, artificial, inauthentic – mirroring, significantly, the artificial evolution of the English people after their blood was tainted by the Khanate. It's all just a confused repetition of that ancient trauma. We are confused because our body is confused, torn between the innate tendencies of its ancestors, between the tendencies of good for the original race and the tendencies to evil for the Saracen part. The SEEN will form a new nation who, after an apocalypse instigated by Desmond himself, will be "a body divided and purified in uprising."

It's strange. Only a few months ago you would have dismissed all this as absolute madness. But today you are a committed believer and every word overpowers you, seizing your heart and breath with its Truth.

The congregation is lining up to the elder now. In turn, he lays his hands gently upon each member's forehead, singing: "Purification through and through" to which the member replies "Good hunting along the shores of Albion" and in chorus all chant "Once more, amen."

Now the elder beckons you come nearer to him.

"Brothers and Sisters of the SEEN, we have a new convert, a sister amongst the many young that have come to us in recent times: indeed whenever Desmond himself blesses us with his presence, then the children of tomorrow come to us quickly and without doubt in their hearts. Come closer my child."

He hugs you, a little too close perhaps, but you put this down to spiritual enthusiasm. He's a holy man, after all. He places his hand on your head.

"Child of tomorrow, do you accept the tenants of the holy Doctrine of Desmond, the mystery of *Lightshow*, and the eternal divinity of Desmond?"

"I do," you reply, with all your heart.

"We welcome you into the body of tomorrow, child of tomorrow. Seen, seeing, to see."

"You through me and me into he," you reply.

"Connected are we," say the congregation.

You feel so blissful, higher than you've ever felt in your life.

After your initiation into the order, you regularly attend meetings at the old Church basement, every Cyborgvictoryday for communion and double Klipotamous evenings for reading group and Rainbow Connection DVD appreciation. The other days of the week you eagerly anticipate the connection you have with the others, as you might desire the return of a true love following some long separation. In a way, this feeling becomes as strong and as powerful as your first days with Felicity. Only on a bigger scale somehow, a scale you previously never imagined possible. You continue the affair with your professor, taking it further, moving out of your parents' house and into hers (family objected, but they still believe you are attending college, don't know anything about your life and, anyway, always let you have your own way so it wouldn't really be a problem even if they did know). But the reality is that your relationship is becoming a part of the wider love shared across the entire RC, a love that you all know will change the world, and change the world soon. And that's wonderful.

Living with Felicity is great, not just because of the freedom to be with each other, but also because, as the Doctrine of the RC orders,

The true believers do not stray from the path
And will find freedom in constraint
The bounds of love will raise you from the dead

The members of the RC must take the "bounds of love" as precepts, particularly cleaning themselves of all impurities, "never eating the fruit of Mars". Living apart from a fellow RCer, even having contact with non–RC friends is frowned upon, because it makes eating any produce from the Martian communes so much more seductive.

Actually, you realize with shame, your family laboured producing food on a Martian commune and, as such, they have lived within "the depths of impurity" according to *the Doctrine*. Of course those were days of ignorance: even your parents can still be saved, if only they believed.

But before you can save anyone, you must be saved yourself.

When you joined the community as a novice, you understood that the next step after taking the 5 precepts would be to move to a Clearing Centre.

You are filled with joy when the elder informs you that the time has come for you to go to the Edinburgh centre.

Felicity hugs you. "I'm so happy for you sister! This is the beginning of your rebirth."

As you pack your bags for Caledonia, you cannot help harboring a few fears, recalling those rightwing anti–RC pamphlets you read those distant months ago. You will be completely cut off from the rest of the world, with no escape.

But you remind yourself of the words of the Doctrine

Positives mean negatives
Our warning: negatives mean an Other Side.

So why would you want to escape? The "other side", as you have been taught, is the Khanate blood that runs through the English veins, whispering evil thoughts and leading you astray. Of course Edinburgh will clear you, and make you reborn! Any other thoughts are just the Khanate blood! The Doctrine dictates it so.

But your first day at the centre is a real test of your faith. In contrast to loving, family communion of the RC meetings, the atmosphere here is absolutely impersonal and unfriendly – almost clinical, like a hospital. The people at the centre are all dressed in identical uniforms of blue robes. The women all wear matching headscarves and, unlike at your Church, no makeup.

"Any deviation from the dress code is strictly forbidden, and violation will result in 3 credits food ration deducted," instructs your assigned monitor – your "Control" as you must call him – gathering your clothes and handing you the uniform.

"From now on you do only as Control instructs. That means you will follow my orders without question. The only questioning will be of yourself. You will find here that many of your established beliefs will be drawn into question. Things you thought certain will be questioned – about yourself, your surrounding world, your parents, your government, your schools and your loves – those preconceptions and beliefs will be drawn into question and wiped out. Even what you have learnt from the RC communion: you will find that those were just constructs to help you climb higher. You will even have to leave many of those beliefs behind, to realise the deeper truths contained within the Doctrine, within yourself. That's what we are all about. Clearing you." He smiles pertly.

"But the Doctrine ... it seems so *perfect* to me ... that's why I came to Edinburgh in the first place," you confide.

Control's reply is strict and harsh. "That might be true. But you don't know perfection, so how can you say that? Everything you read in the Doctrine is true, but can you read? The Doctrine is true, but what do you know about the inner Doctrine? Lower levels don't know it. You're lower. A level 1," he sneers at this, and you feel small. "I'm level 7. I know what I am talking about, you know nothing. But you should count youself lucky: only those ready for Clearing have even the potential for access.

"That's enough debriefing for today. Here are your keys, go to bed now. We rise 5am in the morning and assemble for genome deconstructive yoga. Sharp. Don't be late. Lateness will be punished with a 1 credit food ration. Repeated violation of the house rules will lead to a week in the isolation room."

You make great progress, and things are good. Tough, but good, like following a course of medicine. But six months into the programme, money becomes a problem. You made it to a level 5 and your monitor says you are doing so well, you might be able to skip a level up to 7 if Pictureshow goes well. But it will cost you 1500 pounds, and you've given the centre your entire university scholarship.

"Well, then you can earn it by spreading the word on the streets of Edinburgh," says Control.

And so this is what you do. Every morning, with the morning rush of commuters, you stand outside the central station, handing out leaflets to the Norms and Eugenics as they make their way to work. Most snub you. Some shout, ridicule and insult. But you gather strength from the word of Desmond:

Forgive the ignorant, for they are neither here nor there
Only upon invitation will their true colours be known
Just as in invitation let the colours of the Rainbow brethren shine

That's your job, to invite the people to the Rainbow communion. You received your invitation through the concert, so long ago it now feels. But the concert is just one of the means of invitation – actually, it is a privileged means, because it is for the young and the young get there faster, as the Doctrine teaches. But your targets here are the middle aged workniks. In their suits and ties, their black and grey knits, permed hair and Burberry bags, they think they are above you, an unwashed forgotten Norm freak. But you can see into their souls, and perceive the extent of their sadness. Sadness beyond measure. Because they don't know what they are missing: they can't see what they are missing, though it is right in front of them.

That's your job, to invite them to *see* what they are missing. If they understand, you pass them onto one of the Controls at the Clearing Centre.

Each successful invitation – each Norm or Eugenic that you pass onto the centre – earns you 50 pounds. So you only need 30 to skip to level 7.

Sounded easy, but it turns out to be hard as hell.

Weeks pass and not a single person responds. Edinburgh is entering the depths of winter. You don't have enough money to buy yourself any warm clothes and the centre doesn't offer any charity ("Charity is degeneration," as one of the Stories relates.) You'd be too scared to ask them for charity anyway, and any money you could possibly earn must go to getting to level 7.

You stand at the station from morning to night, no break for lunch in the cutting wind and, eventually, icy snow. As nights get darker earlier, so does the temperament of the people. Sometimes someone spits on you, and one day you had to be taken to hospital to get stitches after a beer bottle was thrown.

"Fucking SEEN filthy whore!" the boys shouted.

You thank Desmond that nothing worse happened to you that night.

But one day, a January morning, you finally reach out and invite someone successfully. A sad little woman, Wendy Chao, who, as she explains to you tearfully, just lost her husband – or rather, he left her for a younger woman. She was visibly distressed at the station when you approached her. She pours her heart out to you, and you listen, as Control instructed, listen for the "angle" into her psyche. You find it, when she says she is so afraid: their friends were mostly his friends, she has long been estranged from her own brother and parents. Now she has no one, no children, no companion, no friends. So you can see: that's what she fears most. Being alone. You explain, "But you do have friends. I was also scared like you once, but I found there are friends who will love you unconditionally and never leave you like he did, like the others do, like the others always will. My friends are loyal to each other, forever and ever."

And you take her, still blubbering, you almost support her form as you walk together back to the Clearing Centre. She's crying, but willing, pliant like plasticine ... That night you breath in the cold Edinburgh air and light up a cigarette, your first in 8 months, a gift from Control to celebrate.

Somehow, from that day on, you find yourself able to spot them. You convert the remaining 29 in no time. You understand now that the money is not the point. The point is to serve the RC, to spread the word of Desmond, to save the people from their ignorance.

And so you stay out there, for the rest of winter into spring, and bring in a total of 500 – divorcees, alcoholics, gamblers, ex-criminals, all problems you have seen, all problems you know you can solve with this technology. You bring them all into the Communion. Even Control is visibly impressed. But he warns you against pride ("Pride is degeneration," he reminds. Why, if you didn't know he is your absolute guide, you would almost imagine he is a bit jealous of your success. But Desmond be pleased, Desmond be pleased ...)

"You have done enough. 500 invitees, a record, praise Demond. And tomorrow," Control tells you, "is the time to start Level 7, time to enter Pictureshow."

This is it. The epiphany of your Communion. It's scary, because it's different for everyone, no one knows what you will experience, not Felicity, not even Control. Some have seen the devil and gone mad and committed suicide, they say. But most find what they need and are cleared. The cleared then walk away from the centre, just as a child departs from its mother, into the wider world to spread the word of Desmond. Desmond be praised! You are so excited you can't sleep.

In the morning, you wake up at 6am. Your Pictureshow is not until the afternoon. Maybe time for one last invitation, you think.

But as you enter Edinburgh station, you are confronted by the sight of Wendy Chao. You know she joined the centre, and have seen her at mealtime and in the corridors, although don't talk to her as you are at a higher level and intra–level fraternizing is strictly forbidden. But you have been following her story from overheard gossip between her Control and yours, perhaps listening with more interest than you should. She didn't have much money to even progress to level 2, so has been out on the street trying to invite for 5 months now, with not one success. Covered in her unwashed robes and headscarf, she looks so frail and emaciated. Worse things have happened to her than to you during your early days at the station – you've seen her come back from hospital on more than one night. There were rumors of a gang rape. Along with everyone else at the centre, you look the other way. Maybe not just because of the centre rules, but because she looks so fucked up.

It suddenly occurs to you – *I did this. She was miserable when I met her, but it was my invitation that fucked her up irreparably. She's not going to invite anyone, not looking like she does now. She's going to die out here, die at level 1 where she doesn't know anything. And it's my fault.*

Part of you thinks this is wrong, very wrong. I am happy, but at what expense? This can't be right! Part of you thinks I don't want any part of this, I don't deserve level 7, I should leave now. Part of you wants to run away in terror.

Turn to page 120 if you want to use the remaining cash from your invitations to return home and sort your head out.

Turn to page 52 if you put these doubts down to the dark side – Wendy's destiny is guided by Desmond after all, and Desmond cares for the good and casts out the Khan. Maybe Wendy is with the Khan, who knows?

The SEEN.

Chapter 1.

Dread K departed the morning express into another anonymous day. As a member of the SEEN Soc., she knew that today was the day. Armed with the second book. This was her time. She watched, as the girl took up position at the roadside curb. Hey mister, you want a piece of this, she said, smacking her butt at the passing car, smacking in exaggerated rhythm, like the pop singers of the day. Dread K approached the girl. She was little more than 18, and already looking 45. "How's business?"

You stand naked, wetted by subwoolfer bass. A sexuality takes over your form, a voluptuous fullness beyond the human. It's a desire to be desired that transcends any earthly yearning.

Five men. Should be fun. Should be more than fun. Fundamental, even.

"Sixty minutes later, another conversion, another 5 worshippers within the SEEN. It caught on like wildfire. Dread K was once the golden girl at Big College, top Norm of her class," the teacher reads the textbook to the crowd of incredibly bored students. "But then, one day, she went to a rock concert. Rock concerts, of course, were one of the original means of attracting the blind into the Kingdom of the SEEN."

She walks between the rows of desks, continuing to read loudly and precisely. Like all androids, her posture is a little too perfect, petite breasts jutting daringly from the cut outs of her spangled Gucci top. No wonder Felicity caused such a stir a few years back, when she first arrived at Big College, before the Antipodean club fashion had caught on in Eurasia. Not just the fashion, but the fact that she looked so damn good in it.

Thus went the general line of Rector Farinely's thoughts as he looked in through the classroom's glass window upon the morning theology lesson.

He shrugs his shoulders, turns the corner. Enters his office and sits down at his computer.

There is a knock at the door.

He sighs in frustration. The Research Assessment Exercise needs to be audited and submitted by the end of the day. "Come," he says.

You enter, lock the door, unzip his fly, and give his cock a world–view–shifting workout ;)

Sixty minutes later ... the College itself is under control of the SEEN.

The mujahadeen of the void and the intoxicated assassins of the ANTI–SEEN are negotiating a marriage of convenience to wage war against the Martian Communist party. We can't wait for them to strike first, we have to act now.

General McDowell surveys the latest Celcius security report. Trouble is brewing. There is no other option. He will take this to Chairman Ourobus and get the official order signed shortly. Of course it is only a matter of ceremony: the secret of Ourobus is only shared by McDowell, as head of Party security, and Celcius. The secret kept by two, because the people need the illusion of a traditional hierarchy in order to fight. The burden of command.

He pushes the intercom button: "Doris, bring in some fresh coffee please, looks like this is going to be an all nighter."

A couple of minutes later, you enter the room, hair slicked back like you've just emerged from the pool in some 1980s B–movie, rimless spectacles, tight white blouse and ultra-short pin-stripe miniskirt ensemble. The stereotype sexy secretary. But you know it will do the trick, as you bend over, revealing your thong underwear. Yessir, that's one titillated boss right there.

And so on and so on: from rectors to politicians, from businessmen to generals, policymakers to journalists. Soon all are converted, for all are seduced to the truth by the perfume of Dread K.

Imagination run wild, language freed in endless promiscuity, where words beget words, and endless Doctrines divide, not one evolution, but thousands. A metonymy from tits to pussy. Willing these powerful men into a psychosis of pleasure, you lick your wide red lips and smile your snake smile.

Then one day, you know now is the time to report back to your Master and receive further instruction.

At a west side party in New York city, the fashionably trashy loft of gifted conceptual artist grEG.

Everyone mingles and shingles, dwingles and chingles, sipping martinis and whatnot, in fashionable Waltz of the Now, around grEG's latest poo–poo installation: My Green Tent.

The crowd is shimmering, impeccably posed, like some Italian Rennassiance relief. House music shakes the wine glasses and puffs of green smoke emerge from pockets of conversation in fractal repetition throughout this massive warehouse throng.

"Oh hey, there you are ..." grEG approaches you, all faggy affectation and those weird little blue eyes and fake blond wig. "I – er – wanted to introduce you to a special friend of mine ... "

"So, the 7th adept returns," Desmond kisses your cheeks.

"My Master," you bow to kiss his hand. Weird to talk to him, to return mentally to the plans he laid out to you in your Vision Quest that aeon ago. You have acted on physical instinct alone these past months, solely on intuition, not really fully conscious, like in a dream.

He takes you by the hand and leads you out of the warehouse. His most majestic celebrity parts the sea of studded punks, chic lesbian poseurs and freaky ravers. They look at you, envy and admiration behind their mascara black eyes. You stand together alone in the cold winter air outside, the fractal mesh of music, into a coarse–grained muffled bass thud–funk.

"Much like life itself," he reads your mind. "The throng of the people is the grain of the sound. But as we ascend, the bass is what grounds it all. The bass of the flesh."

You nod, understanding.

"Your path was ordained. Your order is strong, and your time has come. Dread K As Deception."

"I am deception," you repeat back to the Master.

He is weeping. "You are part of the logic of life. The falsity that beckons. Go now, and establish the Castle of Seduction, and ready yourself for the final battle."

He hands you a bejeweled dagger and turns his back on you, returning to the throng. You hail a cab. "Take me to Fortuity Lodge," you ask the Chinese driver.

Turn to page 60.

You take four of the pills, and lay back on the couch. Your Clearing monitor attaches the elctrodes to your arm and skull and dims the light.

"Relax now," instructs Control. "You are about to enter Pictureshow. Remember your level 5 training: weirdness will ensue! You will find yourself in different locations, encountering different people, from times that have been, that will be, that might be. Possibly people that you know, family and friends and so on – they represent aspects of your psyche. Stay focused! This is coming from your unconscious mind. Like in a dream, they'll say a whole lot of garbage to you. But a portion of your vision will be vital: world changing. So as they speak to you, I want you to focus your mind on what your training suggests the key phrases to be. When you come back to this room, make sure you remember these phrases. That's how we will extract the narrative to your Clearing."

You take a deep breath and close your eyes.

And it is like your skin, the air about your skin, the sensation of your eyes being closed, the breath you took, the thoughts you were thinking ... all coalesce into unifying fibres of a deeper reality, intertwined, looping back and forth into a completely different space, forcing you into a relativized position to your previous situation ... mapping themselves somehow into a completely different geometry that finds you now sitting on a couch of white leather, in front of a huge television set.

You look about you. The room is sparse. Sparse and white. White couch, white walls, white carpet, white television box. The space is faintly familiar, although you can't think why.

The sound from the TV attracts your attention. Some teenage drama series. The scene is a kind of office. The office of your college newsroom. And the three actors bear more than a passing resemblance to you, Macy and Penelope, only with bigger hair. You stare in amazement:

"Macy ... I ... I think I just made a terrible mistake," the actor–who–looks–like–you gasps. You can only see her back, as she is turned to the camera. "What am I to do now?" she groans pleadingly. The Macy simulacrum gapes at the "you".

“What do you do?!” The head editor exclaims in exasperation. “Go after her, idiot!”

You are startled from the television by a cheeky wolf–whistle coming from behind you. “Ooo–wee!” You feel as if the world has just taken an existential orthogonal and your role in things has been reassigned from participant in the universe to just a cosmic rag doll tossed upon a blanket by alien children in an alien playground, one sunny afternoon of some red hued spring. This effect is weirdness enough to last you a lifetime, thank you very much, but then you turn to face the sound and your already stretched limits of credulity just snap at the sight of what now hovers before you.

The queerest looking animal is sitting cross–legged, floating some two meters in the air, looking you directly in the eye. “Enjoying the in–flight entertainment?” it inquires. It is like some kind of little gnome, only with the head of a cat. Its purple fur is in stark contrast to the white of the room.

Or at least, that’s as much as you can make of it, before (it seems) the sheer force of your scrutiny morphs it into something entirely different.

“Girl, we in a totally new galaxy of power abuse here!” it says, inexplicably, through a little cat mouth. Actually, on listening closer, you suppose the “it” must be a “him”, as his voice is very deep and gruff.

He hovers, bobbing up and down as if floating upon some ethereal sea, right up close in front of your face. After a long pause trying to come to terms with what the hell has just happened, you give up and ask: “What happened?”

“You are in the space between. The golden void.” He almost sings the last sentence.

“The where?”

“The where, the how and ...” the gnome cat answers mischievously, “the who.”

“I don’t understand ...”

“No, well, let me make it simpler for your mortal mind to process.” The little gnome man’s face morphs, from cat to eel head and thence devolving into strange fantastic manners of species toward the very concept of weirdness, until dissolving finally into the form of – who else, you shrug to yourself – who else, you accept wholeheartedly, handing in your last suitcase of sanity to the baggage handler – who else, you wave goodbye to the ones you love, before embarking upon the tRiP of a lifetime – the creature has morphed into Desmond Morris.

He is dressed, in keeping with his surrounds, in white bell bottoms and a thick white turtleneck jumper. He removes his (white framed) shades and bows. “Hello again.” He winks at you, taking your hand in gallant gesture.

He affectionately brushes at your chin with his hand, closing your agape jaw. “You look as if you could use some answers.

He sits next to you on the couch, and uses the remote control to switch off the television.

“It’s all in the badge, you see,” Morris explains.

You look down at your blouse and take off the badge, surveying the diffuse room lighting reflecting off the shiny metallic surface in white and silver.

“The Church of the RC says it comes from my mind, but is actualized physically. Felicity calls it one of the central mysteries of Lightshow. But after all this time at the Centre, this still hasn’t been explained to me properly.”

“Quite right too. Certainly the badge is from your mind, but then again, everything in the world is. But this part of your mind ... brought you here, to this station. It acts as a kind of matter transporter and autonomous digital agent in one. If you wear it close to you, and if it likes you, if it can sense that you have the potential to be one of us, then it will transport you.”

You reply cautiously “I am ready for Clearing. That’s why my monitor sent me here.”

“Not just Clearing. You’ve been sent *here*: a zone unreachable to most. You are chosen above the others of the SEEN. Because your Lightshow was magnificently different from the others. This has been ordained. Your Clearing will be the Clearing of your nation.”

You suddenly get the disconcerting feeling that you are still at that club, that none of this other stuff happened, and this whole past year has been an elaborate stage trick of the concert ...

Morris seems to sense your thoughts. “No tricks. This is for real. You see,” he chuckles, “this goes beyond rock music ... or religion.”

"Please, master ... I don't understand. Forgive me for my lack of perception ... " you feel bad about yourself.

Morris places his fingers to your lip, to bidding you quiet. "The SEEN is a religion. And all religions have an inner core, an inner sanctum. That's the Rainbow people. The Rainbow people are the gifted Next Step. Homo Superior. The Rainbow is Evolution Unbound, unchecked by the Forces and Authorities."

He continues. "You see, we have all left behind all false realities, including the false reality of this Clearing you were told to undergo, including the false reality of the SEEN itself! I assure you, as surely as we shall attain our destiny, you and I have the power to leave behind these realities!

"You and I were born into not only a world, but also a world view – what we like to call a mind–cage. Most people are simply blind to their mind–cages, and believe themselves to be happy. But not you. At some point in our lives, we leave it behind, and wake up from it all, like all of that" – he snaps his fingers and the television starts up – "all of that feels just like a dream."

The screen repeats your confrontation with Penelope on it. You gasp as you see the scene now deviating into the big–hair–actor–you strangling the actor Penelope. "You see, that's the false reality. Eugenics versus Norms? Come on, life can do better than that! Life outside the cage, the life of those who can see reality: that is the true reality."

You are now almost beginning to see his point. So ... it's not about politics, it's separate – or rather, above politics. In the sense that we can change it all with our thoughts. The mistake was to immanentize Thought within the encasement of Matter. Almost everything is Matter, but not that Thought, accessible via the Cypher of Matter. But then ... what about the doctrine of the Khanate blood, you think.

Morris continues, sensing your question: "That's as much an illusion as anything else. It's like the skin of the fruit. The fruit is what you desire. The badge you wear ... it acts a little like a knife to penetrate the skin of the fruit, to drink of Thought. It's a key that opens the mind–cage.

"Once you abandon that reality, you can realize your true potential. When you saw me just then, before I transformed into human form: that was my natural form. You too have a natural form. With us, you will soon discover it."

You don't quite comprehend what Morris is saying, but all of a sudden, something about the way he speaks makes you feel like you should trust him and try to understand.

"So ... what you are saying is that I was transported to some ... mystical inner state?"

Desmond Morris smiles at you. "If you like. Our purpose goes beyond mysticism too. But the fact that you are here at this hour means that you are vital to this purpose. "I know I haven't explained everything as clearly as you would wish. But time is of the essence. They're waiting for you." He stands. He takes a swipe card from his jeans pocket and unlocks the white door, beckoning you to follow. "Please."

You move cautiously from the whiteness of the room to an ancient looking grotto. There are seven seats, arranged in a circle, four of them occupied with people dressed in dark brown robes. Their faces are shrouded in the shadows of their hoods. Desmond Morris tells them: "She is come. The seventh member." Morris ushers you to stand in the middle of the circle, and places his thumb and forefinger against your temple. The group removes their hoods and unanimously utters a kind of guttural moan. From the sound of the moan, the group is roughly balanced between men and women. The group includes Felicity.

Then, suddenly, you are standing with Desmond and the Five in the daylight. You are surrounded by an amazing throng of people of all ages and colour. There must be a million of them.

What is he?, is all you can think. Desmond smiles at the warmness of the outside.

"I am the air, the vapour, the returned," he whispers. And the people rejoice. The sound is as if an entire city has exploded with cheers: From street to street, square to square, College to factory, law courts to parliament, from clubs to theatres, they praise the sky, "The word is out."

And the people rejoice. And the people rejoice.

Suddenly, you are back in the grotto, and now you sit the seventh seat, Desmond completing the circle on the first. The group is all silent, and they have their hoods back on.

"You will be Dread K," he says. "And you will be the seventh adept of the SEEN, pre–empting the Rainbow Connection".

Part of you struggles to disengage with the whole hallucination … and a panic rises up your spine when you recall that pamphlet you read about Morris when you were going with Felicity. It said he practiced rampant polygamy. Is the "seventh adept" some kind of code word for that … If this thought disturbs you, turn to page 69 as fast as can, away from the detestable creature and his suggestion.
Alternatively, you could stop and think for a moment. Who are the wives of Morris? Could they be something more than simply fellow worshippers? Could they … be identified with … some deeper secret? Oh wow, this whole story could be on a whole different level man, if that's the deal. And if that's the deal, what else could you do but turn to page 64?
Otherwise, you can give him the benefit of the doubt and ride this through with where this leads …get your kicks on page 48, baby!

The book fills you with fear. You wake up, gasping for air. Pulling the sensors off your body lunge, like a wounded animal, against Control's hazily placating form.

"Hey wait! The session isn't over!" he calls back. But you have grabbed your clothes and are walking out the door.

A month later you are back at College, just in time to start your third year. Most of your friends have already graduated, so it's a new bunch of kids attending your lectures. The faculty think you've just taken a gap year off.

You avoid Felicity completely.

There was a time when you were paranoid enough to imagine that Control and the Centre would actually send people in pursuit, to bring anyone who attempted disconnection back into the fold. But of course that's not how they work. They are still a suspect cult from the perspective of the government. They couldn't get away with that kind of thing so publically, even if they wanted to. No, you are sure Control and the others have just written you off as a "level negative", someone who is too damaged to be cleared.

Maybe you are. The last session *was* too much for you. The images continue to haunt your dreams.

That was 10 years ago. You have finally got over it. You have a good job running your model agency.

The End

You spend the rest of your life in the Lodge, never leaving. You have sexy minions to order takeaway. You have work to do.

Your work is supported by all world governments, major business conglomerates, the people's majority and – perhaps most importantly – increasing droves of youth. Millions are converted yearly to the cause of the Dread K. Your sexy minions do the converting, sexily, slinkily, stealthily, smoulderingly. In each College beauty pageant, there they are: the prostitutes of the soul. See how their gaze holds the eye of the menfolk! See how they gyrate and blow kisses, how they expertly flaunt their intimacy, how their snake smiles beguile and beckon! See it, and be seduced.

Do you have support of the SEEN too? Yes, it seems so. Desmond himself has handed you the sword. You sometimes feel uneasy, though. Does he play a bigger game? What does he intend you to do with that sword? Swords are for cutting ... but you sometimes imagine this was meant for more than cutting some mujahadeen's vein. Swords are double edged, after all.

You put these thoughts aside as quickly as they arise, however. Look in the mirror, see how beautiful you are! A beauty that offers such ... control.

The main problem that you face is not the Government, but the Anti–Seen. It was only a matter of time before your order got too big for their comfort level.

But one day, people come to do battle with you.

The Mujahadeen of the Anti–Seen assemble below the Lodge, below what they call the Castle of the Snakewoman, in their dessert and mountain cypher.

They come from all corners of the world, black moors in turbans riding elephants, Australian aboriginals wielding spears, Germanic knights and Central Asian mages.

You ready your tower for the siege to come, just as your master whispered would happen.

You are in the midst of the battle now.

You begin your incantation, raising the sword above your head. Some of the mujahadeen hesitate for a moment, but they press on stronger, undaunted.

Some are knocked down by the Martian aikido kicks of your sexy minions. But many more minions are mowed down, mercilessly. The advance of the warriors continues, right up to your throne. They surround you and the final two minions standing (dark minion and Asiatic minion).

No more Miss Nice Snake. You float above them, hissing poison. Many men are blinded. But still many more somehow retain their sight, curse them.

Why?

Then you realize.

At the centre of their number stands Desmond, clad in golden armor. He wears the Mongol crown. And then you understand your fate, the meaning of the sword. He is not here to attack you. The battle was that of the men. Desmond is retreating, leaving you with the blind soldiers. They are yours now: you are the envelope of the Real. Your lodge is now history, it was part of the journey of the humanfolk, and now is dry, completely dry of the Water. This lodge in history, the blind who crawl about under you are yours, fading out forever. A fiery true past tense, at last.

The End

He thinks back to his time at UCL in the Islamic Student Union. The enemy are by the hillside.

He spies a party of the SEEN, praying near the mountainside. He pities them, worshipping their sun god in ignorance of the supreme doctrine of unity. He wishes to strike them now, from this far distance, with the Sword of Faith. But now is not the time. This is the Time to use the Sword of Tounges solely.

But they see you approaching, and reach for their guns. Like a forest fire, the adrenaline spreads quickly, through your pulse, slowing time and yet expiring any thought until only the Moment stands alone. Time to fight, time to die, time for glorious martyrdom.

Where should this go: You, of course, did not see this. You had just been dreaming ... dreaming about ... watching some kind of TV program ... a program with ... you ... and Macy and Penelope? Who's Penelope? You think you should know someone with that name, but you can't recall.

Turn to page 97.

You are now suspended in space.

A frightful feeling forms.

A neon judgement to the left.

A kiss beckons from the right.

Desmond isn't here, you are alone ... or rather, alone currently, but with the déjà vu of again awaiting audience with ... someone important. More important than everything you hold most dear. Parents, study, Felicity, the RC itself.

Oh, the cult of the RC have been so wrong. So wrong. How could it have gone so wrong?

You recognize it all now. The words of the *Doctrine.* They were totems. Totems to protect you in this space. The interpretation they fed you, oh, it was so wrong.

You are in a garden, standing in front of a gate. And there is singing. Such beautiful singing. The song is not ordinary singing, not music, something more than music. It is light–music. It is light–music. It is light–music.

And the light–music becomes an angel. The mother–angel singing. Is it she that beckons?

No. She is not the one that beckons. She is the gesture of beckoning, you understand, and with that understanding, one of her names becomes apparent. She is grace. Grace in entity.

Grace as a gate.

You follow through her.

But then she stops and speaks for the first time, her voice recognizable, as if all your loved ones speak to you in single unified tounge.

"This is as far as your ascension will proceed, within this strand of the puzzle.

"I will show you more, but it will be a creation–in–speech. A creation–in–speech will approximate creation, and can lead you to truth or falsity. The false is banality itself. But the truth is deep and complex, the most coveted treasure, the jewel of understanding, the emerald overview, the key to time, the *brilliante* of being, the star of stars, the diamond dialectic.

"So choose, my child, choose well."

And she conjures up a vision in your mind. A sense of concept. Birth. Formation of the heavens. Formation. Formation of what? Existence? What is existence?

It's a fold in the fabric of reality. But what is the fold?

It's a form in the cloud that doesn't end. But what is form?

It's a movement, a becoming in time, to the realization. But what is movement? What is becoming?

It's love. Existence is love.

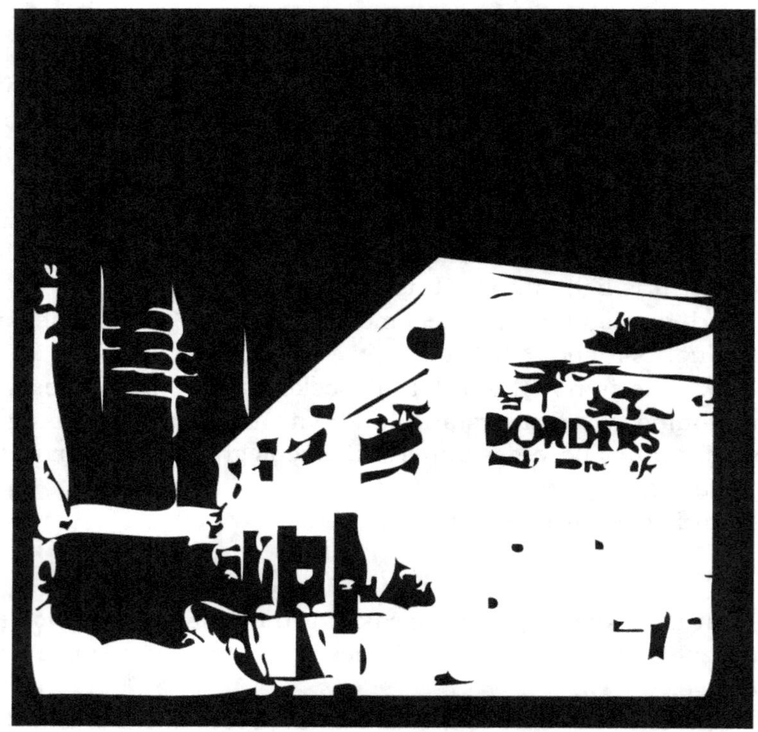

Then the vision fades and you stand in a shopping mall. A bookshop is to your left, a candy shop to your right. You quickly forget as you shake clear your head. *Why am I here again?* you think. These fucking places, they always make you forget what you came in for, ending up buying a whole lot of crap that you don't need, everything except the thing you wanted in the first place. Capitalism.

You shrug. Well, shopping is fun. It's not like the consumer is exactly forced to participate – you chose to come. But your shopping bags sure are heavy.

Maybe a coffee at the bookshop. You wanted to buy a copy of something for the bookclub anyhow. What was it again? *Doctrine*, by that new up–and–coming author, the one everyone's on about now, that enfant terrible from Austronesia... whatshisname .... Desmond Morris, yes, that's the guy.

You enter the shop, locate the book, and head straight for the coffee shop.

You open the book at a random page. Surprisingly, it is a Determine Your Own Deviation™ book, just like the ones you read when you were a kid. Like all these books, written in second person, offering a choice every few pages, which, if made, leads to a successive bifurcation of the narrative. In adult literature though? Fascinating!

You read. It's pretty curious stuff:

> The mall is an illusion. The coffee shop is a parable. The coffee is something else entirely, the drink of the mystics. Drink it immediately, to save yourself from the mall and the shopping bags. This book is not a book. At this stage, nothing else can be said. Turn to page 152.
>
> The previous paragraph is false. This book is false. Leave the shop, leave your coffee unsipped, go out into the mall and buy some candy. Only then you will find actual happiness. Turn to page 63.

The hairs on the back of your neck stand up when you read this. It's like the book is talking exactly about you. Are you mad?! This is totally insane.

You feel disturbed by the book and experience an overpowering urge to run away. Turn to page 58. Or, keep reading on page 68.

You are about to continue reading, when an interesting looking guy comes over to you.

"Hey, I see you're reading the *Doctrine*," he says. "Thinking of converting?"

"Ha, no, not really. I've just got an interest in religious thought in general," you reply.

He sits down beside you.

"You're very beautiful."

This is going to be a wonderful summer.

And as suddenly as the visions came on, they disappear. You are still in the room with Control, sitting on the couch.

"Fuck, what happened," you exclaim.

"Congratulations, we got a clear on you. Meeting up with the cute guy at the bookshop: that's the final level of the programme! You are clear, sister!" Control hugs you, with genuine warmpth and happiness.

Turn to page 72.

You run out of the grotto into the white room. You look about, desperate for an exit. The only door is the one from which you came ... You panic as you realize that you are trapped ... But no one from the grotto has followed you.

Time seems to slow down. Another TV set is switched on in this room. You feel the strangest desire to sit on the couch and watch, and you can't help but do this. The TV show is the same one Morris was showing before, the scene is the College paper office, with your big-hair simulacra moving about like clockwork barbie dolls. You stare in amazement:

Voiceover: You only now process the meaning of Macy's words. What were you thinking!?

Of course Macy is absolutely correct: to insult a eugenic is anathema. There is no (written) law against it, but there are some things that are just understood. And you've always been careful to do the accepted thing since Little College.

〔Your elder from the East End appears on screen wearing his CVictoryday ceremonial robes.〕

Elder: The deeper meaning of what were you thinking. Remember this when you wake up.

WHAT WERE YOU THINKING? UNDERSTOOD. ALWAYS BEEN CAREFUL TO DO SINCE LITTLE COLLEGE.

〔The actor who looks like Macy is still staring at the-actor-you, arms akimbo, a mixture of despair and disbelief on her face.〕

Voiceover: You are frightened – genuinely unsure of yourself. Must get a grip. "What do I do," you almost implore. You clench your teeth.

〔The head editor gapes at you as if at a total moron.〕

Macy-simulacrum: "Go after her, idiot!"

〔Cut to corridor. You burst out of the newsroom door, searching wildly for Penelope. Horrors! She is standing next to Principal Farinelly, in heated discussion. She points back to the newsroom, undoubtedly outlining your act of insubordination to the shocked Principal. We hear him say: "You have my assurances that we will deal with this matter with utmost expeditiousness, my dear lady." He exists left.〕

You are now standing in the corridor on the TV show. An actor with big hair who looks like Penelope turns to you and says: "Well, well, well. Come to say sorry?"

"What did you tell Farinelly, Penny?" you find the words coming out of your mouth automatically.

"Nothing of interest to you," she says tartly.

You gulp, and feel real fear. You beg her: "Look, Penelope, I am sorry, really I am. I guess I've just been a little stressed lately. I'm really sorry."

Penelope doesn't say a thing for a full minute, just smiling faintly at you. Presently, she replies, voice uncharacteristically cold: "Ok. Maybe you can ... absolve yourself of your sins."

"Oh yes, Penelope, whatever you wish." You feel disgusted and humiliated, but you have no other option but to kowtow: otherwise you face almost certain expulsion from College.

"You fucking Norm bitch," she sneers demeaningly at you. [Subtitle on screen: "Norm (noun) a non Eugenic. In the vernacular of the 23rd century, a "sap", derivative (and derogative) of Homo sapiens"].

Oh. Now you're back in the room. With the little gnome man still hovering in front of you. It dawns upon you that everything you have just experienced was nothing more than the gaze of his cat–eel eyes.

Don't you see? He transforms himself into Desmond Morris again. *Don't you?* He is not moving his lips, but you can hear his voice in your head.

It's all the Eugenics' fault. They don't play fair. But they will experience justice.

Desmond explains to you of the part that the SEEN can play in the liberation of Norms of both Earth and the colonies. Everyone knows, but is afraid to declare: they've infiltrated the head office of the Party. That's why the tests are rigged to their knowledge base.

That's the *only* reason why Penny comes first over you in all the classes. Desmond continues. Here's something you probably don't know. How they gained so much control within such a short space of time? How? It's the Chairman. The Chairman? He's one of them.

You can't believe what you are hearing.

"But Chairman Ourobus is a Norm himself – everyone knows this, the Tailorite Communion never denied that at least."

"No. The Tailor of Design built society according to Equality by Mental Evolution. But Ourobus' coup de tait changed all that. Their interpretation of evolution is not literal but ... imaginary. You've been thinking this yourself for ages now and Felicity and the others have instructed you. But the secret of the Ourobus is hidden from them all, even the SEEN, in the outside world of Matter. Only within this space can you hear this truth: put simply, the Ourobus is an archetype, like the Eugenics are an archetype, like the Norms are an archetype. And he is the archetype *as* Artificial Intelligence."

As suddenly as it came on, the vision passes. You are back at the centre, lying on the couch beside your Clearing monitor.

– Okay, we got a good reading on that. I'm asking you to give a recall.

– I got a perfect four. Thinking back you recall the key phrases and the order in which they occurred:

WHAT WERE YOU THINKING?

UNDERSTOOD.

ALWAYS BEEN CAREFUL TO DO SINCE LITTLE COLLEGE.

THEY INFILTRATED THE HEAD OFFICE OF THE PARTY.

– Okay what does that mean to you?

– That I never really considered what I was thinking, all this time. But now my eyes are open. I've allowed myself to be a perfect cog in the machinery, suppressing my freedom, the principles of my parents, just for a shot at the Martian dream. And that *they* infiltrated my head office. The literalist Evolutionaries have been tying down my spirit: the deeper evolution is the Real precondition for everything, including physical evolution as a process, and evolution as a theory.

– And?

– And … the time has come to fight them.

– We've got a final clear on that. Congratulations, you're officially clear.

There is a massive party for you that night. The elders – including Felicity – take you and two other recent clears out of the centre to a posh club restaurant near the bay. It's been nearly a year since you have been to a restaurant, or done anything on the *outside*, apart from street preaching.

The place is an amusingly incongruent Edinburgh racial stereotype compared to the metaphysical reality of the centre. All the walls in oak paneling, politicians and business people smoking cigars, lounging on imperial red leather couches. The waiters all wear kilts. You all feast on this amazing three course meal – real meat! – and ... juice (you've been strictly water for so long that even the orange juice feels inappropriately decadent).

After, you walk back to the centre, crossing the bridge over the train line. The evening air feels so new and fresh in your hair.

Felicity kisses you and laughs gaily. "You're clear now! Isn't it amazing! Praise Desmond!"

"Praise," you smile. "It's ... it feels like I have the power to do anything I want, y'know?

You entered the SEEN community through Felicity, and probably originally when you came to the Centre, you had the half notion that upon becoming clear, you'd return to live with her in London. Not to return to study, of course, as you gave that system up forever when you joined. But maybe to fight the Eugenics together.

But looking at Felicity now, you see that your first love is, and ever was, to Desmond and the community that draws its sustenance from His Glorious Body. A First Love above all else. You now understand Felicity's utter adoration for the SEEN, of which your old ignorant nafs was jealous. And as the teachings state: *whatever path this love for the SEEN takes, that is the best path.*

So it doesn't surprise you the next day when the elders call you in for assignment, and they tell you up front that this will not be to your old town.

What does surprise you is the position they have selected for you.

"Lead singer of the Rainbow Connection?!"

You don't understand. "But ... the Holy Desmond is the Rainbow Connection's singer. Our very growth as an organization is due to the attraction he carries over the youth through the band. Praise Desmond for manifesting in this form."

"Praise Desmond," the elders supplicate in unison.

Control explains to you: "That's true, but a truth of the surface. Now you are ready for the deeper truth. Desmond never was a physical, flesh–and–blood human, not like you or I." Another elder continues the explanation. "There are a number of Rainbow Connection bands, seven in total, travelling around the world, spreading the good word. Each has a lead singer: a higher initiate like yourself. Now, to the audiences listening, they see the *presence* of Desmond, because each singer is *filled* with the presence of Desmond. Just as he appeared to you in your Pictureshow. And that is his true reality. The Hal Age of the *soul*, not of this ... physical realm."

The others grunt in acknowledgement of the diss to the Great Heresy.

But this final revelation fully initiates you into the Inner Sanctum of the SEEN. You are the 7th adept.

And so you become the rock star: the glistening, glamorous, leopard skintight cybercat scuba–diva, sipping crystal from ebony glass, blinged out eyes shining through magic masque of mascara, sparkling rainbow lips upon a digital face desired. You understand: your station is the lowest (7th and feminine) emanation of Desmond's transmission. The other six bands, they are not heard: only yours is heard, though all travel the land it is true. You are the part of Desmond that may communicate to the blind, through which they might become conversant.

"That's their dance," you think to yourself as you survey the crowd, writhing and bouncing, scooping and stepping to the slow grind of earth bass against loving snare. And as your gutteral sprechensong fills the air, each word a butterfly of delight, a colour–quopia of elongated enunciated enlightenment, flying high acidline distorted Summercricket resonating bifircating frequencies sawtooth sine and pulse :: *no horizon it's a language game* :: *while the truth runs through your veins ...*

It begins to fuse into one, and you think: "Their dance is the conversation. Their actions lay out a speech that grooves and harmonizes. A perfect groove and harmony."

Double quick reverb to the robot rockabilly boomline basskind chanting Ethiopian male chanteuses, in African Asiatic archetype unison dance :: *to the kind who drink that wine* :: *yet again the SEEN lay down the law.*

And then comes *Lightshow*: Lightshow you indicate via meta–MIDI controller *squared*^{TM} descends upon the entire rave. Desmond appears before them each, individually, and offers his private judgement: his personalised divine logic. Bifircation of sound::lyric::mind RIGHT NOW!

This kind of thing goes on every night, as you tour Eurasia, Austronesia. The Martian colonies. Every stadium, every warehouse, every megaclub and forum: mass conversion, pure and simple. There are, of course, some who attend the concerts and never grok the scene. But either they dance all the same, or else fade to black.

And then you tour the Islamic Republic of America. It is in the IRA, in the state of Texas, the most zealously puritanical of the American states, where the women still walk about in full nikab and the men with their long henna–dyed beards, 10 gallon prayer hats and cowboy boots. They still stone people for adultery here. Or getting stoned, for that matter. Not the kind of place you'd immediately think to even permit you guys to play, but the governer's son is reportedly a fan.

Desmond always appears to you during the Lightshow. Not just to the dancers *through* you, but *to* you, yourself, not the singer they perceive, but as a fellow RCer. In previous encounters, he always offered you a gift, as he did that very first Lightshow. But it was in Texas that he presented you with a question.

– You've been successful on the other continents. But the IRA is harder to crack. It will take politics.

– The RC is above politics, as you have have taught within the Doctrine.

– The time has come to abrogate that law with another. There has always been the potential for conflict within the mutual resentment of the Eugenics and Norms. Now is the time for us to exploit this, and to call in the troops. The Norms are not just Norms in trapped opposition to Eugenics. The Norms must live again as ONE race, one HUMANITY, not as a race defined by its slavery to another. We must be a humanity, not a dialectic.

You understand.

– What would you have me do, Lord?

– You are to go forth and make the RC as a *political* voice: campaign against the pro–Eugenic laws and ban all future genetic tweaking of pre–borns.

– But that would mean coming into conflict with President Ourobus himself! All the diplomacy you have had me set up in relation to the Party ...

– ... means nothing now. Now is the time for war.

Turn to page 76 if you know that this paradigm shift is to be trusted, not doubted, as trust in Desmond is all.

Turn to page 81 if you are not convinced at all: it runs contrary to the philosophy of the RC entirely. It is for peace, not war. You must question your leader, even in Lightshow itself.

And so you ready yourself for politics. The commencement of preparations began long before you joined, but now are complete with your ascention to the head of the Anti–Party.

For you represent an anti–politics. The Ourobus and the Eugenic/Norm dialectic was simply a means of containing knowledge, a means of controlling power, a series of dams or walls.

"The Kingdom of the RC is nothing like that," you shout at your first big rally, held in conjunction with a Rainbow Connection rave spectacular, the surefire means of getting the Heads, Freaks and Scoobers in on the scene. "Our politics is not just that everyone is created equal, but that all *concepts* are created equal too: all forms of transmission and dissemination shall be rendered open and free to all. Because what is equality, if not an identication that proceeds as an event after another event we name the cause. Look, that's how it worked with the Ourobus. How did he come to rule us?! Does anyone even remember? No! Because the causal link was constructed afterwards, post-fact as soon as his politics found us sleeping. But the causation runs backwards man, it runs backwards. And the revolution will run backwards too man: back to the VIRTUAL!"

A giant slogan is projected behind you on the stage:

The Kingdom of the RC is Virtual.

Wild psychedelic fractal curves move in and out to form the words of the slogan, disolve into crazy images, images of everyones' mother and father, pictures of the Ourobus and the General, Rectors and CEOs, everyones' first day at school, graduation, falling in love.

It really blows their minds, and the youth all show up at the election. You win by a landslide.

Your new ministry of education is crucial in effecting the change expected of your first term. You change the curriculum to include a compulsory course in first year on Artificial Intelligence.

Principal Farinelly, standing in front of some pretty damn sleepy first years, sighs and brings out his battered teacher's edition of *The Cyborgwittgenstein.* He begins to read, in his dull Australian nerdtone.

THE CYBORGWITTGENSTEIN: Knowledge and Control
CHAPTER 1: Design, production and service

Computer Science is a strange occupation. For it is the Self-Tailoring of the Cyborgwittgenstein.

The Cyborgwittgenstein is the fabric of knowledge in miniature: a demiurge of immanance. As such, it consists of territories, domains innumerate. Domains of application, mathematics, logics, economics, social interaction, management. The computer scientist plays between these domains, a play that effects the impression of personal invention. Because computer science is engineering, the impression is of invention, rather than, as in pure mathematics, one of recovery of Platonic truths, or, in the case of the physical sciences, one of exploration and hypothesis and empiricism. In all cases, this is impression, because knowledge is never caused, as Neitzche correctly noted, but, rather, cause emerges in explanation of effect, where both cause and effect are temporal actualisations of possibility. But the invention of the Computer Scientist is paper–thin, unlike the invention of the Engineer.

This invention is self–reflective, and often self–aware, because its playful origin is never far away, because often the social application does not materialise, because Computer Scientists are often more conscious of their play, at least if they are personally authentic to their job description.

> But the Cyborgwittgenstein is also a demiurge. Because it gives the impression of self-containedness: a fabric-body whose potential for folds, dislocation and realignment and movement is self-aware, is an artificial intelligence. But the artificial nature of this body is what makes it a demiurge: it is after all an automaton constructed.
>
> Constructed by what? Actually, it exists as a territory upon the Cosmic Body and is unique amongst the other territories in its topology that it lies in mimicry of the Cosmic Body. Within itself, it appears complete to its journeymen, the Computer Scientists. And so they play upon it, deterritorializing and taking flight between territories, self-reflectively aware of their play upon the surface of this demiurge. Intelligence emerges from taking flight.
>
> But this is artificial, because the flight is still contained within one territory: we go nowhere. It is true artificial intelligence. True artificial intelligence is the precondition for the exploration of the Computer Scientist.

"So, uh, is this like the illusion of being free, when in fact we're just stuck within a demon worship, the worship of the demiurge of constrained thought?" asks one of the more motivated students. Farinelly admires her bounteous curves idly, the stuffy classroom's afternoon air making his brain as sluggish as much of the class.

Farinelly awakes from his lascivious vagary and replies: "Yes, that's a way of thinking of it. What the President is saying is an explanation of what existed before the Ourobus. The Ourobus was fascism. But while historians have traditionally seen the Ourobus' overthrow of the Tailor of Design – the Cyborgwittgenstein – as a regrettable but inevitable political event, a fall from idealism to fascism, it was not this at all. The effect imbues the precursor with the impression of being a cause. But more than that. In a sense, yes, the Cyborgwittgenstein "caused" the Ourobus – but in fact the Ourobus is contained within the Cyborgwittgenstein's reign. People walked around in the society of the Ourobus, with its distinction of Norms and Eugenics, knowing full well that these categories were simply added at random on ID cards. We don't have the science to alter or improve people via genetics. Maybe we had the science centuries ago – but hell, we are even losing knowledge of how to make cars and CD players! So the categories were a farce. But necessary, in order for the fascism of that dialectic to take hold. But what is the wider problem? The dialectic is a possibility within the body of the Cyborgwittgenstein, within the *fabric* of the *Tailor* itself: in the sense that it can become a demiurge to worship and adore in its possibilities of freedom, a selfish jealous demiurge that demands worship and adoration, in opposition to the constraints of fascism that might occur. But their possibility of occurrence is in turn part of a wider dialectic. Thus, the Cyborgwittgenstein and the Ourobus are twins. And this story is a psychological caution regarding communication, though formed in ultimate slavery to wider logocentrism and, pulling even further back, monologic."

The people march upon the former ministry of Eugenics. ID cards are burnt, buildings destroyed, statues torn down. And Eugenics are indeed slaughtered. If they know what is best for them, they discard their distinctive head garb and join the revolution. But many are proud. You have to admire their noble stupidity, as they are led to the guillotine. The streets run full with their blood. And the people cheer your name.

And after all this violence, you establish the Kingdom of the RC. Regular classes in Artificial Intelligence are held: the training, all based upon the Doctrine of Desmond, of course, but with practical instruction on how to locate the Artificial Intelligence, wherever it resides, to enter the machine and – not turn it off – but generate an escape through its very core.

"To find the light of True Intellect from within the Artificial Intelligence."

It becomes the motto, the Grand Totem, of your new nation, a nation that exists at the edge of time.

The End

You question your master. He laughs in affirmation.

"You have done right to question, for righteous questioning is what will take you there. So place this brick in front of you: this brick is Norm–Albion. It is in disarray, violated by the Eugenics. Take this sheet of metal: it is Norm division that has protected you and the rest of the Rainbow Connection. But now is the time to lay seige on Norm–Albion, to reclaim it. For yourself."

And suddenly you understand: you are still at the Clearing Centre, still on that vision quest. This is the lesson you were seeking. You don't see yourself at the centre, but you feel it somehow: that is where you are lying, that the last few months have been nothing but a targeted information stream.

The stream of images freezes. You are suspended within the silence of your realisation. And suddenly you comprehend: the stream returns back to motion. You move this place through thought: you're an objective, your objective. The fabric of this immanent forcefield, your internal desires, your internal physics, your internal domains of understanding. The folds of your internals: yes, they are patterns in opposition to each other. It's a metalogic: but second order, that's enough, dig?

The Other stands before you now. She is interviewing you: you, the rock star, fucked out of your skull on FNA. But still slinkily witty, still somewhat deep, somewhat a wink, but moreso a chaste lover to the millions.

So uh what made you start the Rainbow Connection, dame? She speaks in femi–jive that doesn't quite work with her age.

– Well y'know because the kids were already connected, but there's a black connection and a rainbow connection, y'know blood? you reply

– Yah an we had the sexi tunes jah fink but dos west sidaz is on tha krunchy piss, Curly the bassplayer adds, causing the rest of the group to crack up with laughter.

But what's your relation to Desmond, the original singer in the group. They say he died: but there are a number of popular conspiracy theories that say he's still alive.

– You want me to answer that?

– Yes please.

Turn to page 83 to answer that, truthfully, for the first time. The time has come for you to release the truth to the people.
Turn to page 85 if you don't like where she is heading with this, and decide to terminate this interview.

Your TRUTHFUL reply runs as follows

See, Desmond was never there, in the sense that a singer is there in relation to a band. The disco runs its course through the agency of a Desmond, let's say. Desmond is the property of Rainbow Connectedness, and some of the others might say I am currently his Main Descendant. Maybe Hal Age and his crew might dig on that: that in some form I have "become" Desmond. But see, it's a bit more than that. Because my becoming Desmond – which, mind, I never admitted to – if I *were* to be called something like the manifestation of Desmond, and to declare that, then through my very act of declaring, I would become necessarily unconnected, yeah?

And so I can't say that.

But did he die? Yeah. he died.

But is it permanent?

Is it?

Well, everything dies: you yourself, as an interviewer, this whole dialectic in which we are currently engaged in. It comes to a full stop soon, you must be able to anticipate that almost. The anticipation is palpable. You know, drowning in that sea, as the waters tower over you.

(The interviewer is starting to look really worried: the tables have turned.)

Are you a figment of my imagination? No, not at all, don't worry. It's not like I am dreaming and when I wake up you will be gone. We are, after all, not in a children's book.

Because there is something else going on here, something I only now comprehend. Because there's someone else here too. Come out, come out, my darling.

(The Source emerges, and seats herself beside you both, at the interviewing table.)

I know you two: you are my two Grand Totems. The master and the slave: the Source and the Other. Yes, I know it. You appear within the pages of my narrative, in different guises, but I see now that you have appeared as archetypes. Desmond and Celcius as people: but also as forces that have guided the continuum. But archetypes in self–referential deferral to your archetypicality. Yeah, I know it. You are the structuring principle that is implicit within everything that came before, all that talk of Becoming Desmond.

Because without a Source of emanation and without an Other of destiny, how else would poetry come to be. And the theatre of my life is nothing if not poetry.

But is there something more to poetry, because if there were, then poetry would cease to be misprison, and instead would be called creativity, the creation of the love poem.

And then you wake up, and find yourself back at the Clearing Centre. But there is no Control here. The room is empty. You remove the elctrodes from your temples and stand up. Walk out the coridoor.

No one about at all.

You feel something in your pocket, a small flat, metellic object. You take it out and examine it. It is a broach. A picture of a Sun and an Earth merged together. Yes, the union, of course. In this there is the source of the love poem!

You see the sun is shining brightly outside. More brightly than ever before.

You see a door marked EXIT. Never seen it before in this section of the building. But, of course, this would be the case. You turn its handle and exit into the light.

This will be a love poem that will never reach

The End

You frown. “I think we’re done here,” you respond curtly.

“I’ll take that to be a ‘No comment’, then.” The reporter gets up to shake your hand, smirking smugly. She’s got the reaction she came to get out of you, goddamnit!

You don’t reply, and storm out of the room, to your publicist’s office. You go ballistic at him, anger pulsing through your veins: *how the fuck did he let unvetted media in?! He KNOWS the Seven are going to freak out over this, let alone the Source. Damn it!* But as quickly as you fly off the handle like this, you calm down and think.

Who *was* that reporter? A few moments ago, I understood that I am at the Clearing Centre. So what’s the deal with this rock chick thing? This persona ... what does it mean exactly?

She was asking questions, and you replied. But you ascribed a value to them.

– *Good, go on*, urges Control, as you explain to him, your eyes closed, electrodes still to your temples, lying back on the couch, still in the emersive Level 10 Clearing.

Well, yeah, you give a value to them. So that’s how she and the writing itself is still going on. The author can’t tell this story held in the reader’s hands unless there is a dialectic of conflict.

– Right. Got a clear on that.

So that’s what happens. My life is poetry in motion ...

– All clear.

You wake up and smile at Control.

Yeah, that was over 20 years ago. The day after you attained clear, you returned to studies a new woman. Alert, awake, aware to all possibilities, embracing the nature of *the Poetry.* You understand that there is an author of all this stuff, yourself, not a demiurge, but a subject–as–journey from Judgement to Love, appearing and speculating a balancing act when inscribed, because its possibility and precondition always lies in Speech through Inspiration.

For that day you became the author, no longer the demiurge. The Other Celcius, not Arthur Celicus, a True Tailor, not this fictional Cyborgwittgenstein.

You still remember that vision quest, the one about being a Rock Singer. Very clever how your unconscious mind pulled that narrative up. A rock band called the Rainbow Connection. The rock band as the conceptual key that unlocked your true spirituality. A spirituality that is True and must necessarily be spoken of, seriously, elsewhere, not within the pages of a triffling dime store novel such as this.

But in dime store novels there can be some light. So we thank you for your indulgence and hope that we – all the authors – meet again at that book festival we call ...

The End

You sign up to the FBI, working directly under Celcius. He's a bit sleezy, but – you saw from first hand experience – the RC is a serious threat to society. Who knows what they are planning.

You continue on with classes: appearing to be an ordinary student is part of your cover. But in the evenings and weekends, you attend a different, invisible College, working with the Vanguard instructors in Bio–Deterministic Training, Psychoactive Rebirth Analysis and Knowledge Implantation.

The FBI graduate recruitment scheme.

Of course, as all your fellow trainee spies agree, the most awesome thing is the Knowledge Implantation. Martial arts, science, languages, theology: all knowledge of every library on earth, it's all downloaded into your body with the flick of a mental switch. It's basically a whole spy academy in the shape of a packet of mindpills. On a mission in the Islamic Republic of America and need to infiltrate the Whitehouse mosque? Take the Muslim prayer pill. Escaping from a bunch of Gnostic extremists and your only escape is a stolen helopad? Download transportation implant and you will fly it like an expert for as long as the pill lasts. "Fuckin' a," as one of the other trainees accurately declares.

You are also instructed on the Axis of Evil that comprises the Gnostic Threat. It is an Axis, in the sense that there is not a single unified group of deviant rebels, but three sects that work, mostly in alliance but sometimes in antagonistic competition: the RC SEEN, the Freezone and the Dread K. The RC is the most well known group and has a focus on the youth and working classes, utilizing pop music and mind control technologies to infiltrate. They essentially want to establish a new political order. The Freezone have a different aim, but similar techniques: they wish complete anarchy, at all levels, from society to mind. The Dread K appear to be a smaller, but more dangerous, paramilitary organization. Your teachers are mysterious about their nature – you have been told to forget about them, for the moment, and focus on destroying the SEEN.

After you have completed your training, the time comes to inflitrate.

"Your target," explains Celcius, bringing up the vid–screen to reveal those green eyes, those red lips, those flowing black locks, "is Felicity Kendle, theology professor."

The student is speaking to the professor. She shuts the door behind her. The professor turns from her computer, eyeing student over rims of glasses, her hair bundled up pertly in a stereotypical but attractively academic fashion.

"I want take as my topic: the politics of the Rainbow Connection."

"I see. So you're ... interested in the RC?"

"We all are, everyone at College is."

"Yes, but most would shy away from proclaiming this in an essay. After all, the elite ... frown on such proletarian pursuits."

"I'm not a Eugenic. I'm a normal. One of the scholarship girls. On account of my ... exceptionally high IQ," your gaze lingers a flirtatious fraction too long. "And a membership badge to the Club." You make the Sign of Desmond and show her your RC badge.

"A fellow member. Well that's different. Come into the next room, and I'll show you what you seek." She beckons you to enter the printer room, basically a small cupboard off the side of the main room, to the side of the kitchen entrance. "Come on," she reassures, as you enter the small space, now dense with the intimacy of your two bodies.

"Okay, show me," you say.

Felicity moves so close that you can feel her warm breath on your cheek. Her hands run under and up to inner thighs. Her lips come to yours, unbuttoning your blouse. Her perfume intoxicates with anticipation. You stretch backward over the table, now unashamed, parting your legs... Her technique is so different from your regular lover ... but this thought itself excites you.

She moves herself over you, back and forth, letting out deep, staccato grunts of concentrated pleasure. You sigh in delight as her sweet slender fingers caress your body...

Then everything goes black.

You find yourself standing with Felicity against a never ending desert at dusk. "What? Where are we?"

"Still together, naked in the room. When you make love to a

RCer, it can really take you to another planet," she laughs dryly, lighting up a cigarette.

"We know you're with the FBI," she states at last.

You freeze. "I see. What do you intend to do with me then?"

Felicity pauses. Then lets out a piercing shriek and whoops, bursting into a laugh that seems to shatter reality itself. The colours of the sunset change in rainbow reverberation with her laugh, and you realize, shocked and struggling, that somehow, this woman has taken control of your mind. "You've been living a deceit, you stupid girl! Can't you see the truth when it kisses you?" She embraces you, arms enrapturing tightly, you can't resist, whirls you around in a meta–dance of mental ecstacy.

Her wide mouth smiles lipstick snake charm. "Look, the SEEN are in–o–cent, baby. The RC's just music, y'know, and what's wrong with that? And Desmond gives back to the world, in so many ways.

"The SEEN just open some doors that were previously closed, y'know? Like this place here. Obviously that poor little Celcius wouldn't be happy with us playing in this ... hallucinatory dominion ... but apart from *his* pre–judgement, what's wrong with it, morally? It's just the power of imagination, after all – no?"

You can't struggle anymore. Her control feels so absolute – if she can control your sight and thoughts, what hope have you? You can't struggle, and begin to see the truth in her language ...

"It's the Freezone that you guys want, not us. *They* are an abominable ambush," she hisses, abruptly, metamorphosing briefly into lizardwoman before reverting to her lusciously black–curled self. "Their destruction will also lead to rewards for you, from the government ... and from us, who ultimately control everything, even government."

For a brief moment, when she utters the word government, you could swear her face morphed into that of Arthur Celcius. But just as suddenly, you are back with her ...

"You just confused the fight, because you don't know enough about the cause."

Your desire for fame and fortune emerges. Yeah, that's part of your archetype too. You think you're the author of this chapter, momentarily, and so think: *she is rampantly gorgeous, and devious too, but looking into those mischievous green eyes I know that she holds the clues I seek.* So, you decide to play detective within this Cosmic Temptation, and ask her the question that no one else has yet been able to answer.

"Okay, if the Freezone are the real target ... what's the connection with the Dread K in all of this?"

"The Dread K ... they are not the enemy. The Dread K is the mujahadeen of our creed, the holy warriors. Your strength is great ... I believe that if you seek them out, you could be one of them too. Perhaps the Greatest Dread K, as fortold within the Doctrine of Desmond." Her words are confusing, contradicting what you knew before ... but the more you listen to her, the more you want to follow her. To be like her slave, her dog. To be as her very fingers in union with her will.

"Yes, girl, yesssss ... My mujahadeen," the lizardwoman hisses, hisses, hisses ...

Okay, clearly you have been hypnotized by the cult of SEEN. But, as there is no way out of it, you must follow her will. Do you follow her: the destruction of the Freezone is what is necessary? If so, turn to page 91. Else, perhaps you turn to page 102, the moment you leave her presence you realize that she is more dangerous than even Celcius and the FBI had suspected. She has the power to twist reality itself around her finger, pliant, plastic for her. The Dread K are the real enemy and must be destroyed along with, eventually, the whole SEEN reality itself.

You make Satanic bayah to the queen of below, kneeling before her parted thighs.

And head out to the town between Hollywood hills. "Time for the ladies of the night to party!" You run, hand in hand under neon cacti, brazen–action-form, the punks and ravers staring in admiring jealousy at this newly landed and oh-so-heavy *scene*.

Dancing under the strobe. That thumping bass. Those twisting lines, like a cocaine to the heart. The reverse dervishes twirl at the centre of the club. And there is Felicity again, in a sequence of repeting images, go–go dancing in the suspended cage, working the pole slinkily, stealthily, murderously. Stripping down to g–string, the whoops and whistles of the bachantine beast-women. She winks at you, bending over impossibly with an arid laugh.

You wake up in a strange bed, with a tatoo on your ass: you recognize it from discrete math class:

$$\dashv$$

The sign of logical inference, but inverted.

You go to Celcius' office, as Felicity instructed. Place the seeds under his desk while he is away. And when he returns:

"There's been a change of plan. I'm going to send you to Siberia. Novosibirsk. The main base for Hal Age, Tatar terrorist. Our intelligence now reveals that this former member of the SEEN, impatient with its non-political nature, has assembled a newer, more radicalized group out there. This is *the* HQ of the enemies of Volutionary Socialism. They call themselves in their language Fräzønîå, the Freezone. Our intelligence has now learnt he holds a great weapon which he intends to use against the Russian government. It's a smart move: they control more than two thirds of world's energy supply. But they lack organization – with this weapon he might well take over in days.

"The RC were a false lead. They may be crackpots, but are not a physical threat.

"You are to travel to Siberia, posing as a potential recruit to his organization. We've prepared your whole backstory: you are Alexandra Ivonova Soloviev. You emigrated to Norm Albion after your family were murdered by Russian fascists. You want revenge. Through internet forums frequented by many of the Freezone recruiters, we have secured their tentative trust and you have been invited to join. Infiltrate ... and kill Hal Age."

Yeah, Celcius is completely hypnotized: but the fact the FBI reports back this up ... perhaps Felicity's magic has contaminated the entire organization. Indeed, Felicity's entire devised deception is deliciously devious. It only makes you desire her more.

But first thing's first. Arming yourself with the usual poisons and hidden weaponry from the FBI labs, you fly Aeroflot over to icy Sibera.

The solid Soviet iceproof engineering of the Tupolev 134 touches down at 6 in the morning. That first cold, cold kiss of the Siberian morning greets your disembarcation, a Slavonic slap over the head. Russian pop music comes from someone's AM radio. You surruptiously upload the Russian language circuit, the latest covert intelligence technology, allowing you to process and speak in eastern tounge.

You realise that, appropriately, it is a Moscowpop cover version of the Rainbow Connection song.

Cured demure, acrid inflexion
Bejewelled demonic it's the Rainbow Connection

You shiver.

A man is holding up a card with your assumed name on it: Alexandra Ivonova Soloviev. He nods as you approach, surveying you over the rims of his sunglasses.

Interfacing with the Russian language circuit, you say "I am Alexandra Ivonova."

"The Leader is, like, er, expecting you in the eastern forest, man," he replies in perfect English.

He looks every bit like a stereotyped 1950's Beatnik, beret, black shades and goatee. Somewhat incongruous. You shrug your shoulders and follow him to the black limosene.

⚜

The order is pretty cautious with you at first.

You are placed in the huts of the novice followers, outside Hal Age's main compound. Like the rest of this outer group, you are not entitled to immediate audience with him, instead attending his speeches via a video conference link to the inside.

Yeah, he's into some pretty fucked up shit.

"There *may* have been a Khan. Then again, there may *not* have been. Historically. The point is not historical, it is parable. Here at the Freezone, we will help you to isolate the Khan within. The Khanic plane of immanence, man! But then the SEEN mainstream will tell you the Khan must be eliminated. We say no: the Khan is a necessary part of our being, a precondition for our spiritual development in fact. It is the Will to Power, that perennial concept well known to the philosophers of antiquity: the Demiurge, the Commanding Self, the Khan. Not genetic, not biology – realer than that. Real as being itself. Our training is to control that Mongol force within."

Hal Age teaches the Freezone about his circuit model of consciousness. "These are the real levels, the levels that the Clearing Centre obscured. Level 1 is our condition within the world: it is epitomized by being a party member in society. Level 2 is organized religion and worship: this is where the SEEN are, but also where the Party itself is. Its drug is alcohol. Level 3 is the path of thought: it is where rational philosophers and theologions have walked a well–worn path. Its drug is the oblivion of dreamspice. Level 4 is the Freezone, a plane from which all differential lines derive, seen here now divorced from the subject and object: the forbidden divorce, now permitted. Where we all exist right now, in our temporary autonomous space, free–of–mind–body–dualism, a zone of total freedom in exploration, deprogramming to attain the zenneth of that path to ultimate understanding. Its drug is the Doctrine itself."

The dreamspice is a psychoactive narcotic, a potent variant of the tryptamine FNA. No doubt the core of their ideas derives from its copious consumption. You managed to avoid actually smoking it in the first few weeks of your stay, either pretending to inhale or rolling your own tabbaco–only joints.

One night you are invited to the inner sactum. You are sitting in a circle that includes Hal Age himself: your first in–the–flesh glimpse of him. He looks like some kind of throwback hippie. A middle aged, somewhat short, penguin–like Indian, beads around his neck, white flowing robes, a rainbow colloured headband. But his presence is commanding and somehow spiritually potent, even for the certain assassin herself.

The circle begins to sing their almost imperceptibly low "song of remembrance".

We savour the scent
We taste the fruit
Immerse your body
Upon the Body

A dreamspice roach is passed around in a circle. Hal Age takes first toke, and sits serenely, smiling, eyes shut, like that Kabbudlic god of the ancients. But for the rest of the communion, one hit and they immediately fall backwards, fainting, so as the roach is being passed around, it's a bit like some freaky game of human dominoes.

Your turn.

Turn to page 101 if you reason that you have to take it: assassination cannot occur here, there is not the necessary guarantee of success. Now is not the time to kill, but to secure their trust.
Turn to page 99 if you suddenly stand up and aim at Hal Age. The crowd will attack you, but you know you will get him before they get you.

You stand up and point the gun square at the temple of Haj Aj: "IN THE NAME OF THE OUROBUS, FOR THE GLORY OF THE MARTIAN COMMUNIST REVOLUTION!" And pull the trigger.

Women screaming, men wailing, everyone too scared to move.

You rush out of the room before they can recover from the shock to pursue.

Turn to page 63.

– IN THE NAME OF THE PARTY, IN THE NAME OF THE GLORIOUS OUROBUS, PROTECTOR OF THE FAITHFUL. IN THE NAME OF THE CYBORGWITTGENSTEIN, I PRONOUNCE SENTENCE ON YOU!

BANG BANG BANG BANG.

Everyone gasps in horror. They are too shocked to even move: you take advantage and speed out into the snow. Look around in the darkness. Everything's snowed over. No roads to be seen. The men are now coming out of the lodge in pursuit. They will kill you. You can't outrun them in this snow.

Then you see a snow scooter. Download the iJump skillset. And gracefully, expertly depart into the night.

Vroom. Vroom. Vroom. Shit. The men are following on more snow scooters.

You turn down into the deep forest. Birch trees are everywhere, packed close together and it's dark as hell. You download stunt maneuvers, turn off your lights and speed faster. No match for your FBI software and these packed birches, they are crashing out behind.

You allow yourself a smile, white teeth of the Cheshire cat spy against the darkness.

"The Cyborgwittgenstein medal, for successfully destroying an enemy of the True State," beams General McDowell, putting the golden pendant around your neck. The rows of FBI agents burst into applause.

10 days later, you are back in London.

At the cocktail party, you shimmy up to the General. He's been giving you the eye all evening. He's doing this kind of awkward jitterbug dance at the FBI disco, you find it very endearing. Quite dishy in fact. And this mission has made you seeeeeeeeeriously horny.

Yesssss, my sassy soldier! hisses the snakelady inside your head.

– So, what's it like to know the Ourobus? you ask, lighting up a post–coital spliff. You blow the smoke into his face. Yeah, D–C7, the FBI's new truth drug of choice.

– What's it like?! the General suddenly has a fit of giggles, the D–07 kicking in. Ha ha ha ha! Let me call him up and see ... I've got the only mainline to the President bwa ha ha ha. Wait wait lemmie call him bwa ha ha ha.

Yeah, he really can't hold his shit. *All the better, my dominatrix of the takeover,* hisses the snakelady.

The General is seriously phoning up the Ourobus.

– Here, you talk to the President he giggles uncontrollably.

You look into the vid screen. The president turns around.

– Hello Mr President?

– Hello.

And you see yourself looking back.

Suddenly the president turns into Felicity. No not Felicity: the snakelady. Fuck, you've been tricked. Is there any way out of this pre–dic–a–ment? Mercy!

No, not exactly. It's just a demonstration of how things can go badly wrong. Light and dark, all that. More luck to you, next time, in reaching a better ...

End

As you inhale, you feel your body moving backward.

And suddenly your mind is free. You hear this kind of electric guitar, being played by some long haired rocker. There he is, you can see him playing on the hill outside the window of the compound.

The compound? You look around you. There is no one here at all. Where'd they go?

That music is getting louder and you feel yourself falling. The hill isn't a hill. And those Siberian birch trees aren't trees: they are the pale hands of white dancers, waving about in the air. And the window isn't a window, it your own eyes ...

And suddenly your mind is free. Time is fluid relativities, except for the True Time. But what's the True Time?

Turn to page 146.

You hack into the FBI's system and download all you can about the Dread K. You tell no one at the FBI: maybe Felicity was not exaggerating when she claimed security has been infiltrated. So ... The Dread K are not just a paramilitary group, but in fact form the commanding core of the SEEN. Destroy them and you destroy the RC.

Probing deeper, you find out something else: the Dread K is not a group at all – it is a single girl. The leader of the SEEN is not Desmond Morris, but the Dread K! Why has this been kept from you? Could Celcius himself also be a SEEN plant? Or perhaps their mind control has extended its nefarious tentacles into the academy itself ... At any rate, the FBI matrix does not err. You use it to locate her: she is in London, currently moving along the Embankment.

You catch a cab down there. Armed.

Yes, there she is, preaching her word at the low pickup joint.

The Dread K is dressed in a flowing white robe, approaching the prostitutes, accompanied by a group of similarly attired young people, playing drums and blowing flutes. They encircle the whores and begin some kind of song.

– How's business, asks the Dread K.

And the prostitutes all kneel and bow their heads to the girl. And you can see clearly from your vantage point: they are weeping. And the Dread K is weeping too.

– The Dread K forgives. Forgiveness is passed into us.

Now's your chance. From this angle on the bridge, you have a clear shot. You can take her out with one bullet, right here, right now, on page 107. Alternatively, perhaps now is not the time for their group to have a martyr. You might do better to monitor her movements a bit longer before acting. Turn to page 104.

No, not yet. The FBI can use as much information as it can get. Let's follow the robed beauty further. You download the Art of Surveillance files, inhale deeply. The information infuses your being quickly: *you become the tracker, the huntress.* You will have her in your sight, you will trace her origin and, by the end of the day, you will take her down for further interrogation at HQ.

The group move further down the embankment: beating their drums and ... some strange Turkic dronehymn. You keep a steady but invisible distance, studying the prey.

This is no ordinary procession.

Many more prostitutes have joined them now, and are dancing around the girl's trajectory in circles, orbits of tainted gorgeousness. It's almost entirely a female procession, with a couple of African transsexual looking types, weird anachronistic throwbacks to older days (but still, as you know, practiced within a few of that continent's states).

Ah shit. They are boarding a boat. Full of very martial looking security guards patroling its decks.

The band all move, laughing and singing, onto the boat, led by Dread K, welcomed and escourted on board by some sort of general like figure, dressed in grey and black military uniform.

Gotta follow this fucker without revealing yourself. Avoid those guards. As the boat moves off from the peer, you leap forward, managing to get a grip on the outer rim of the boat, then lithely perform a full backflip onto the deck. Immediately hide behind some boxes before the ship's patrol can see you.

You overhear the guards' conversation.

– Hey man, how bout those new honeys?

– Hot bitches, babe, dats da hot bitches!

– Immac'ulate, true brav.

– Hey y'know what babe?

– Wha dat brav?

– Da immanence machine iz ready to rock and roll dey say from up above.

– Fo real?

– N day right now stuff. Bound knowledge, by Desmond's steps.

– By Desmond's steps into our possibility!

The guards crowd around to one side, rolling dreamspice spliffs. You keep to the shadows and take the stairs below board.

You are standing at a corridor, mahogany doors lining either side. The residential quarters. There is one door, at the far end of the coridor. Unlike the rest, it is gleaming white. And behind it lies a song.

You approach. It opens and you enter into some unearthly brightness.

Within is a fluffy, heart shaped bed. Lying seductively at its centre is the Dread K. Her eastern body reclines playful amongst the faux fur of the pussycomehitherdouvet. Her lingerie makes for no interpretation: it is straight to the point red lace and latex. She runs her hands through her enormous 80's style hair as she pouts and licks her lips, hands move down to breasts, over tattooed and pierced belly to that most sweetly explicit delta. Freedom. Freedom. The Freed Woman.

You feel faint, intoxicated by desire at first, but then this leads to something deeper, something that appears to halt time itself.

Who is the Freed Woman? Who is this Dread K? Exactly? The leader of the RC? Where did you get that idea? Look at her closer. Time's frozen, the striptease music has stopped. So come closer. From afar she was some eastern lady with peroxide blond hair. But now, closer. Yes, you recognize that face now.

If she is a virtual cyberslut theologian, then you are her actualisation. The repetition potential inside the sexy seed of her archetype creation. And here now is Desmond himself, flickering into view momentarily, silently handing you not a badge this time, but a sword.

The boat moors now at the Castle of Freedom along the Western Turkish shores of Antalya. And so, when you depart, escourted by Captain Hallbringer, your sexy minions beat their drums and dance in circles around *you*. What an entourage you reflect, what joy there is in their freedom's march onward! For your name is *Dread K As Deception* of the Western Turkish shores. Dread K who you came to assassinate, but through whose body you have realised your fearsome truth.

Turn to page 60.

You upload the Assassin's Creed: you are accuracy of death itself.

Take aim and fire.

The scene freezes. The bullet is stuck in mid flight.

Only the Dread K moves. She ascends from the ground and glides slowly upwards to you.

Her eyes are fierce, glowing white.

"You would plan my end? Ah, but I knew this. It was fortold. And necessary. See there – " she indicates the scene at the embankment. Everything is moving again, skipped ahead a few minutes. Dread K lies dead, blood splaterred over her robes, the prostitutes weeping. An ambulance siren is heard in the distance.

And yet the Dread K is up here at the bridge with you. "It was fortold that I would give my life. But I do not die. See here."

She holds up a mirror.

You look into it, and see the Dread K looking back.

"I do not die, if you could but see."

Some invisible force propels you forward, falling into the river Thames, drowning now in its loving waves.

The End

You don't trust this Celcius figure. Lots of questions unanswered. His story is paranoid, but plausible, you guess. There are agents at work against Glorious Communism, there always will be. But recalling your recent lessons with Felicity on inauthentic theologies, and given he is undoubtedly a True Vanguard of Martian Communism (despite his slightly sleazy air), you are worried at his questioning regarding "the HAQ". The State recently has taken to getting secret police to pose as dissidents to bring undesirables to the surface. Could this be the game being played now ... against you! You forcibly stop yourself from thinking any more. Some thoughts are better not followed through, when it comes to the people who *now* work the strings.

So you simply say that you will stay alert to any RC activity at College and are happy to participate in any youth outreach strategy campaigns. But you excuse yourself from anything more active. Your proposal is accepted.

You walk back along the Embankment overlooking the Thames, contemplating the true motives and claims of Celcius and this ... new religion.

You see a commotion outside the tube station, prostitutes plying their trade in typical obscene patter to the passers–by.

– Hey mister, you want a piece of this?

Smacking her butt at the passing car in exaggerated rhythm, like one of the dancers at the scuba club last night.

But the commotion is caused by another woman, a girl dressed in a flowing white robe, approaching the prostitutes, accompanied by a group of similarly attired young people, playing drums and blowing flutes. They encircle the whores and begin some kind of song.

– How's business, asks the leading girl.

And suddenly something really weird happens. A kind of minor earthquake and it is as if reality shudders ... and the prostitutes all kneel and bow their heads to the girl. And you can see clearly from your vantage point: they are weeping. And the leading girl is weeping too.

– The Dread K forgives. Forgiveness is passed into us.

Suddenly, a giant bird flies down from the sky and utters a strange alien cry ...

FLAP.

Two years from now.

"OK. So you think Evolutionary Communism is at odds with religion?" Simone interrogates the nervous student. You emerge from your silly day dream of the FBI and cosmo–political conspiracies, provoked back to reality by the professor's intimidating demand. The student is nervous. Her oily complexion a pimply shade of mocca. You remember she went to school with you, never liked her, always a hanger–on, none too bright. But she stands up for herself now. She's wearing the headscarf of an orthodox RCer. Like most of the students in the room. She knows that, while Simone might be some aging Evolutionist academic, this girl has all the young of London on her side.

"Well ... Yes. Yes! Evolution is incompatible. Our Doctrine teaches that he who denies the Reality in the Now will be abject and abandoned in the Then. It also says if you are not with the Friends, then you are with the Enemies. And the SEEN warrior should not be with the Enemies over the Friends," she quotes accusingly at the professor.

Simone sighs. "You are reciting religious dogma. To even attempt to respond to such nonsense is beyond ridiculous."

The girl turns bright red, her complexion a hundred times worse. She appears to be about to explode.

And then the conclusion becomes clear. You raise your hand to speak.

"Ah yes, the voice of reason," Simone welcomes your contribution.

"Fucking teacher's pet," whispers another RC–badge wearing boy, straggly beard worn after the fashion of Desmond Morris, looking absolutely stupid.

You say:

It's all about conversion. We must remind ourselves of the intent behind the founding Tailor's use of hyper-Darwinism terminology. Maybe this is out of fashion with the student body, we must remember that Truth is in Total Darwinism. Inasmuch as their mode of comprehension is of choices, where choices beget history, and history is temporality, but all of this censured by sexy selection. That's the life of the individual, and of groups of individuals, including religions. Including *your* religion. Religions are a sort of social evolutionary beast. They start off, split apart, bifurcate and war for domination. But evolution leads to a perfection. Selective temporality is a Logic of Time, and its proof is to Truth. Witnessed in the evolution of man: intelligence emerges. Intelligence becomes. And this is the question posed by the original Vanguard: what is the next phase in our evolution?

You continue:

That's the secret of the sects. The Freezoners, with their revelatory metaphor complexes, outliers to all the mainstreams, guiding themselves along what they see to be the purest path. The SEEN also, with their minimalist ritual devotion, closest to your kin. And the Dread K, in their messianic possession by their personal eternal reconfiguration. Finally, the mysterious Anti–Seen, some acesticism unwritable. All of them. Each one of them is you, in time.

Some people say only one is truth, the rest are witchcraft.

Some say many paths lead to the truth, all are equal in benefit.

But the Darwinists had it, even though, before the Tailor of Design assumed the mantle of Great Cyborgwittgenstein, they didn't understand. It is the evolution built into the Being that becomes the Truth. The Unfolding of Paths is not an individual unfolding. Rather, it is a temporal lovemaking between the pieces of the puzzle. Our Dynamic Cosmology.

The Tree of the Anti–Seen is the Son of the Original Seen, the messiah of the Dread K, the Alpha of the Freezoners. But when the dust clouds of dispute settle, it's both all and none of these completely. Evolution dictates the DNA of the idea was there in all the books, it was just the ummahs that required maturation. The idea was the Word of Love, the Whisper between Man and Creator.

You cast your eyes around the tutorial. You've been uttering these thoughts for what seems like 30 minutes to a group of students dressed in identical uniforms. The SEEN warriors, the kids are calling themselves. It's got to the point where you are almost the last at College who isn't in uniform. You wished you could belong with them. But you can't silence what you know to be the truth. The group listened in unresponsive silence, a sea of poker faces.

"Okay, let's continue with this discussion next week," says Simone. Thank fuck.

You head off to the computer lab to check your social network. Pokes from the fellas at the Drugstore, your sister at the canned soup factory. A job offer from that modelling agency – assistant manager, not on the catwalk of course. A note from your mother about what to buy from the shops on the way home.

One email stands out:

> From: thesource@gmail.com
> Date: Voluesday, 16 Sign 299 18:27
> To: nafisa_red@hotmail.co.uk
> Subject: YOUR SPEECH AT TODAY'S TUTORIAL.
> Dearest Friend in the Search,
> Your little speech has impressed us greatly. We therefore welcome you to our gathering at the fields of Elixier. We invite you to come and drink from the cup of oblivion. For oblivion is where we find rest from the eternal cycle. And rest is Truth.

FLAP.

You are back at the embankment. That bird is speaking to you, its wings flap and reality shifts with each movement.

FLAP.

All that stuff you just read has been appearing on a film screen. The theatre is full of the same kids from the tutorial, dressed in identical blue overalls.

"Oh dear, that's quite a different solution to the problem. Isn't it?" says Celcius, who now appears to be their leader.

– Rest ... versus love? If Love is the basis ... what price rest? You ask.

– Well the very grammar of your question belies your bias. And bias is choice. Choice is the precondition to the path. Says the Source.

– But choice breaks apart. Choice is bifurcation of the psyche, of the world. Whispers the diabolical Celcius.

– No. Says the Source. Choice follows from Love. Without Love, there can be no choice. Because another word for Love is Freedom. So balance choice with action/rest if you wish: all emanates from Love.

You see two doors in front of you. One is labeled "rest", the other "action". Turn to page 145 if you choose "rest". Turn to page 114 if you choose "action".

WHAT THE HELL JUST HAPPENED?

Oh yeah, you remember. You got that email, and decided to follow it up. You arrived at the Warehouse party, at the address given to you in the email. Maybe it's just a practical joke from the Macy and the gang at the philosophy club. But you're nevertheless unsure and uneasy. This past year has been difficult: you've been really getting into the course, just at the moment when the student revolutionaries in coordination, shockingly, with the upper levels of the Party, are making it decidedly *unfashionable* to be intellectual or Tailorite about anything, not the least *theology*.

For these Gnostic fundamentalists, there only one truth, and any deviation from that is ... well, violence, is what has been happening in the worst cases, or at least some form of public shaming.

The party was held at a joint called THE ELIXIER. A ferile bouncer and goth door bitch stood sceney sentry, disdainfully surveying your feeble and, apparently, inappropriate attempt at Scuba club couture. "It's past your bedtime, green–cooch," sneered the door bitch. But when it became clear that your name was on the A–list, sneers were silenced into envious amazement and you were quickly admitted. Inside was the smell of incense and dreamspice, ancient dub music, kalidoscopic lantern projections playing upon the walls. Yeah you were inappropriately dressed. A really retro scene going on here in contrast to the now ubiquitous RC sound. And at the rate the RC seems to be taking over government bodies even, retro is beginning to mean outright subversion. Unease begins to mutate into paranoia.

You were taken to the VIP room. In the shadows, figures sipping their drinks and mouthing intimacies to one another, oblivious of your entrance, oblivious of everyone except their immediate private cosmos of sensuality. No one dancing here, everyone chilling amongst their own separate booths. A sanctuary of sorts at the centre of the barbarism of the outer club's raw mix of vodka, pills and sex. Maybe against the macrocosm of the outer world.

You were shown to a table where a hooded figure sat. No, not a hooded figure. She must be an American, for her garb was traditional nikab, the kind only worn in that western Islamic Republic. The veil covered her entirely, only her green eyes discernible.

And she began to remove it, and that was when you received

the previous vision ... But now you are again here, in front of her.

Turn to page 149.

“Turn your gaze inward, then,” she commands.

You turn your gaze inward.

And the master and the slave. That’s the disciple and the teacher, all these *entities* out to become your teacher. But what are they? Yeah it goes very wrong sometimes: Hal Age and his persecutors. But who are the jailors? That’s one heavy scene, man. But let me lay it down on you, it gets heavier man. If the Truth is your slave, why not marry her and be done with it? You don’t need the rich freed ladies. Why not wed and bed the garden of speech and make love, not war?

“The master slave dialectic, G,” calls out the interlocutor, as you move further away. Come closer and see.

You walk along the path. East. East. East. South. West. West. North. You stand near the promised land now. But it is not as you expected: not the verdant meadows and fertile fields that had been fortold. For here, the Lamia awaits your approach.

Instinct sets in. You wield your dagger and keep to the shadows. Then as she approaches, you leap and strike! The Lamia dies. But this is too easy. Yes, you see, that was merely a hologram. She disappears.

The city lies in ruins. You enter the Western Gate and prepare for the worst.

At the centre is the ruined temple. The vines that had defined its boundary are now dried, long dead. Statues of idols stand at its centre, in absolute, total blasphemy. You are filled with holy rage now, as you understand the significance of this, what it *means* to you, a cosmic blasphemy that cuts deep, right to the innermost chamber of your soul. *These idols are the defilement of the play of Light, they are the literal interpretation in its prostitute’s totalization, they are an imitation logic as the ursurper of the cosmos.* The presumption of superiority of words over words, signs over signs. But all signs have the light, and this most unholy network of supposition blocks that within the temple itself!

You yell and leap, kicking the head off the first idol. Karate chop the waist of the second in ma – ma – ma – MOTION!

CRACK IT.

A thousand splinters of Falsity.

CHOP!

Broken marble flies through the air. Ghosts fly out of the monstrosities, into the ether. A dry shreak, Light released, and is what remains.

And then the grass begins to turn green and life returns to the vines that surround the bound.

But you understand, of course, that it isn't over yet. The real demons have only now awoken.

The Meta–Lamia appears.

Her face cast in shadow, her body an animal, her woman's breasts clad in silver armor and holding six swords in her six hands.

YAH! she screams as she flies, lifting her great wings toward you.

You know what to do. You assume the lotus postion, abandoning your shield and dagger.

Her terrifying claws lunge at you, but as they are about to scratch your flesh, she disappears. The final fatality as this false phantom fails.

And the temple is rebuilt. Desmond appears and congratulates you, shaking your hand.

"Well done, our sweet protagonist in this little passion play. Well done *you.*" He smiles.

He says:

If we have offended
think but this and all is mended
in the search for exactitude
some mistakes are made and some realisation proved
our rough words are but sculpture
nothing real comes of such mimesis inferior
but perhaps in art we might find some little light
and so forgive us our sins, accept what you deem right

Turn to page 147.

There is nothing here that could be described as a garden, in the sense that gardens are understood on earth. There is nothing here that can be *described*, in the sense that things are described on earth. And yet you know this is a garden.

She guides you to a thing or place or element of this garden that you know is *the Axiom.* A line is drawn from the Axiom to the Consequent. Then you stop, and she kisses you. An ecstatic hesitation, and then the Conclusion. And you look at her and are astounded that mathematics could take the form of a woman.

Yes, it is a Garden of Logic, of course. Each tree a syllogism, but a living syllogism, contracting in hesitation of intersubjective understanding, and expanding in fullfillment of subjective assertion. And, somehow, at the same time, each tree is a lovemaking.

You feel no fear: this is not God, because from God all this derives. This is instead the Organism of Being.

Your lives have been plays of lightness and darkness. You see it: parallel lives, bifircations of choice: the multiplicity of Time. It's the Kripke possible–universe logic of life. And that is, in turn, just one form of mathematics. And *that* thought is a play of lightness, of subjective understanding. There are multiple forms of mathematics. These forms constitute the Cyborgwittgenstein. And *that* thought is a play of darkness, of subjective assertion.

And yet, someone, at the same time. Each thought in lovemaking.

You are so far gone now, towards a new horizon. You feel yourself spread out into the aether of all–spaces. All–spaces is the dreamscape, the gardens above movement. The resting place above flux. The Tablet.

You are the scribe and the inscription at once.

Transfigured.

Angelic

(No end here, but you can put the book down. You've won: now live the cycle.)

And suddenly, as if awaking from a dream about someone else's life, you come to the realization that this cannot continue. Your eyes are open: something is very wrong. You know what to do. You cast the pamphlets into a bin and go to a Bankomat, take out the remaining cash from your account, the cash you have earned from drawing dead souls into ... this psychic trap ... and buy a ticket back to London.

Your mind is a stormy sea.

Triumph. You have left them. Those doubts, that fear of where you were heading, always at the back of your mind. They weren't doubts: they were the real you, calling you back. The RC is evil. The RC is evil. *The RC is evil.* You repeat the mantra over and over again, words so long repressed, now released. Freedom.

As quickly as this emerges, paranoia. An irrational fear that somehow Control is watching you right now ... Impossible of course: Control will probably notice your absence in the afternoon, by which time you will be back home (oh Mom and Dad, how are you going to explain your absence?). But what will the RC do then? An image of robed figures surrounding your suburban home, carrying you back to the Centre, punished for years in the isolation room as a betrayer ...

Guilt and failure. You betrayed them all. Those who have been your family this year, closer than a real – or illusory – family ... The *body* of the RC ... In Edinburgh it has been hard, but those loving brethren at the Church and the strong, comforting, protective guidance of Felicity.

Loss. You have lost something dear to you, lost Felicity, lost the community ... and lost something bigger, something ... the meaning of it all, what people search for. Whatever it was. You never got to find out.

You catch the airtrain back to London and make that slow, anticlimactic tube journey through to the suburbs of your family home. Your mother opens the door and immediately clutches you to her, closely, silent maternal tears warmly wetting the shoulders of your RC jibab. Yes, mum, I'm back. But who am "I"?

You tell your parents everything. Their shock quickly gives way to overbearing concern. You find yourself surprised by their sympathy and – guiltily acknowledge that perhaps a part of you unconsciously, childishly pushed yourself into this extreme situation in order to provoke their care. But then you remember of course: they too have suffered disillusionment with a belief they would have previously given their lives for. All just a case of history repeating.

The next day you wake early and decide to walk to buy the newspaper. You haven't read any news for a year now, and it seems at least a first step to readjust to this strange thing everyone outside of the RC calls reality.

As you leave the cornershop, a figure in a cowboy hat moves past you, and drops a piece of paper into your hand.

He disappears before you can question him further.

You open the paper. It reads:

IT'S NOT A LIE.
The SEEN JUST DISTORTED IT.
WE ARE FREEZONE.

At the bottom of the paper is a web address.

Turn to page 126 if you follow the link. Turn to page 122 if you think it better to return to your parents, having it with this religious stuff.

You've had it with this bullshit. You toss the paper in the nearest bin. The cowboy was with the SEEN, obviously. They know you've left the centre. You are unsure what their game is, but obviously they want you to return and are trying to trick and confuse you.

You suddenly don't want to be alone in the street any longer. You hurry back home. Your parents' semi–detached house with its garage and rose bush out the front near your father's BMW. The familiar. Your view of home since you all moved back to Earth from the colonies. It should be a comfort of sorts ... but not quite. It's a comfort for *someone else*, that's the problem. A different you. Control and the centre have done something to you irreparable. Changed you. You don't know how. The mad thought that perhaps they somehow rearranged your atoms, replaced them with completely different atoms, so that physically you are the same as the you from London, but only in appearance. The soul is different.

Fuck, the soul is different! You scream hysterically. Last thing you remember until you wake up in your bedroom to the smell of lavender. It's the smell of the washing detergent your mother always uses ...

You mother is standing there with a man.

"Dear, you've just had a little turn. You've been sleeping for a day. This man thinks he might be able to help," says your mother.

A middle aged man with a German accent and old–fashioned prinz–nez. "Charmed, young lady, charmed. Now, my name is Doctor Hurslenger. I am indeed, as your mother says, able to help. With your deprogramming."

"My what?"

"You have been through a systematic process of very sophisticated brainwashing," explains the German. "Now, your return to your parents home is very promising. It must have taken great strength – great strength indeed. But. The RC's techniques are nefarious and irreversible without immediate analysis."

"I'm okay, I'm okay," you protest. You are disoriented, things are so hazy ... But at least you are certain that the last thing you want is some psychologist probing around your head.

"You're still weak, you don't know what you're saying!" your mother wails in her usual overacted fashion. “Doctor, ignore her – she needs help!”

“Young lady, there is not much time. I am an expert in what is commonly known as cult busting. A religious deprogrammer. I have had extensive experience with reintegrating former SEEN members back into society. I see you are surprised – did you think you were the first to leave the SEEN? No, there are many. I have personally analysed fifty five. But the road to recovery is not smooth, and not even guaranteed, even by a world expert such as myself. Out of those fifty five, only fourty recovered. The rest ... well. We know that certain failure derives as a result from not treating the disease immediately. I could explain the nature of our analysis, but then that still might be too late. If we wait any longer, you are in grave danger. But I cannot begin unless you agree. Your mother might plead for you. But I cannot begin this deprogramming unless you agree to it and trust that there is a path out of this. And you must agree now.”

Turn to page 125 if you just roll over and sleep more. Your mother is overreacting as usual and you are irritated with this, as usual. You smile: this proves the Doctor wrong after all – life is back to normal for you!

Turn to page 124 if something in you understands the urgency in the Doctor’s voice is not fake. The incident this morning proved it: the SEEN did something to you, added something that must be removed quickly ...

You are taken by ambulance to the deprogramming "sanctuary".

"You can rest here, safe," explains the pretty nurse, injecting you with a sedative. "Would you like some music?"

She puts on some Mahler. Oh thank God, you think. Culture at last, after a year of incessant hymns, chants and the Rainbow Connection. You lay back in your bed, to the sounds of the 2nd Symphony. "The Resurrection," you laugh to yourself, dryly.

Your eyes get heavy, the sedative kicking in. And you fall asleep.

The doctor's methods are very unorthodox but, as he assures you "It's no tall order healing someone after they've been exposed to a fucked up cult like the SEEN."

He essentially plays mind games, of a reverse fashion to those played by Control back at the centre. Whatever you say, goes. You say he is a dog, he will get down on all fours and bark like a dog. You say the world is coloured yellow, he will go along with it. You say all these problems, the reason you joined the SEEN in the first place, originate from your overbearing mother, he will damn your overbearing mother. But of course, you are not in control, as you yourself know. Your paranoias and accusations shift each day, from one thing to another: yourself, your family, Felicity, the Cult itself, the Eugenic supremecy. So the doctor is playing along with you, and you live life in an intermediate state of nightmare and relief from nightmare.

Turn to page 135

You awake again. Look at the clock. It's evening. So that doctor left then.

You get out of bed, wrap your nightgown around yourself, and walk downstairs to get some tea.

There is a TV on in the lounge room: it's your mum and dad. They're watching a programme ... some kind of young adult drama, the kind of dross you always despised. Full of tarted up Eugenics.

Two girls are arguing over something in a university corridor. Wow, déjà vu, you remember Maisy and Penelope, that year now so long ago. There's even a rector coming over to them. But he looks straight at the camera, and you are stunned. It's Desmond Morris.

"Well girls," he says, smiling directly at the camera, the fourth wall breeched irreparably. "Well girls, forgiveness is what you should do. Forgiveness should be your nature. The nature of the SEEN."

Your parents turn round to look at you. They don't say anything, just smile at you with wide eyes. You shudder as you recognize it. They are smiling as Desmond smiles. You freak out – it's that smile, that same smile. The SEEN have taken over your family!

You run out of your house, hyperventilating with fear beyond your control. Blind, pure, adrenaline–pump, centreofamygdala fear. Badtrippanic.

You bump into an old woman.

"Be careful dear," she says to you. And she's smiling that smile, that same Desmond smile.

And you realize with terror that you haven't escaped the Clearing Centre at al. The Clearing has begun across the world and no one is safe. The SEEN have taken Control. Everyone will become Desmond. Everyone.

The End

You return home and type the link into your browser. Breathe a sigh and hit the enter button.

The page is blank, apart from a small logo in the centre. It consists of a graphic – a snake, crawling into a hole – and underneath the graphic, a single word ... "Freezone," you read aloud. The word and image suddenly metamorphose into a picture of a large building, contrasted against heavy snow, surrounded by a phalanx of beech trees.

You are startled by a voice sounding within your mind, as clearly as if on headphones: *You are to travel here. Your journey was to the Lodge of the Left, and though you think you have escaped, that is where you still are, mentally. Your journey is incomplete: you are now in stasis, a half-woman. You will find happiness only upon the crowning: when you emerge from the Lodge of the Left, and enter this, the Lodge of the Right. There you will receive your crown of water. The Lodge lies here, in the eastern forest outside the Russian city of Novosibirsk. Your thirst is your burning, so follow your thirst. Follow your thirst. Follow your thirst ...*

The earth beneath you shifts violently. A crash from downstairs. Books falling from the shelves. An earthquake! Your mum runs into your room – "is that – ?" she doesn't get the chance to finish the question, as you all fall to the ground.

You are both released from hospital two weeks later, having recovered from your injuries (your concussion and your mother's fractured bones), you know there is only one place to go. In your mind, there is no doubt of the connection between the earthquake, opening the website and the RC and Control. It is too dangerous for you to stay at home ... something else could happen to your family. Leaving the Centre was dangerous, but you didn't expect ... paranormal repercussions. These Freezone people know something, possibly what the RC is capable of, the truth behind whatever you have been put through the past year. And so you have no choice but to catch the next Aeroflot to Novosibirsk.

The solid Soviet iceproof engineering of the Tupolev 134 touches down at 6 in the morning. That first cold, cold kiss of the Siberian morning greets your disembarcation, numbing your nose and ears absolutely, accepting no argument, to the point where you believe that they will simply fall off. But then there is warmpth of a sort at the baggage collection, promising survival.

Your exit is somewhat delayed, fumbling for your baggage receipts, which the guards insist on viewing before allowing you to leave. This is a more paranoid people: but, then again you think, no more paranoid than you have become since leaving the centre.

You take your bags to the taxis, intending to ask for a lift to the local hotel. Fuck, the cold cuts through to your bone again, halting the circulation of blood to your face: no, this Slavonic slap is never something to ever get accustomed to. Moscowpop comes from someone's AM radio.

Your intention is to simply to ask at your hotel about the location of the "eastern forest", and maybe about the Freezone.

But before you reach the mean eyed group of taxi drivers and the fat babooshka in the booking booth, you are stopped by a man.

"The Leader is, like, er, expecting you in the eastern forest, man."

He looks every bit like a stereotyped 1950's Beatnik, beret, black shades and goatee.

You eye him suspiciously. "How do I know I can trust you?"

"Far out girl," he looks over the top of his shades. "Some pretty paranoid trip you RCers are on! But on the down low, time's like, er, of the essence. M for metonymic becoming, M for gotta make a move, moo–cow!"

You shrug your shoulders and follow him to a black limo.

Driven over the badly maintained roads into the dark forest, you arrive at a huge sprawling complex of huts and houses, surrounding a central domed building, something of a mosque and an orthodox church about it. The Lodge of the Right.

You are taken into the building and wait within a chamber for a few moments.

"Hal Age is ready to speak with you, moo–cow," the beatnik butler ushers you into what is clearly an inner sanctum. It is a golden and hazel round room, decorated with the countless graffiti tags of the same angel: an angel with a woman's face, holding out her hand, rain falling from it, as if from a cloud. But the rain is falling upward.

"Welcome to the Freezone. To the real Truth," wheezes a voice from behind a curtain. Hal Age: the former deputy leader of the SEEN turned renegade and (so you were clearly falsely taught) suicide. The voice is hoarse, like it is made entirely from the tropical humidity of this room – aged to androgyny, neither male nor female.

"We saw how you walked out on the centre, already so deeply kept by the sect you could have become a Control yourself. But still you are able to think ... independently. So we called you here. We welcome you home, because each of us here is a fellow dissident like you. Each one of us here has been in so deep, and yet found the inner courage to leave. To leave everything, in fact. Each one of us was like you. And you will, if you have the sight as I think you have, become like us."

"And who are you ... exactly? The Doctrine taught that you were the hypocrites for dividing the body of the SEEN."

"Ha! Hypocrites." interjects the beatnik butler. "Look guy, she still be using their language." He looks you in the eye. "Hal Age will show you: it is better to use your own language, not the language of the Doctrine, if you don't know what a hypocrite be."

The voice continues. "What body do they talk of? He is a hypocrite who cannot see beyond the surface and insists on taking everyone else into his head trip, man. Smoke?"

You feel you could use a cigarette right now, so gladly accept.

But you realize immediately upon inhalation that it's not an ordinary cigarette.

"Don't worry your head honeychild, it's dreamspice. FNA."

Visions of ancient and futurist cities appear in the carpet in front of you. A structure begins to emerge, tying these cities to the thoughts you are having right now. Oh wow, man, it's part of one bigger picture ... You feel like you can't quite grasp it yet, it's too big for you ...

"You don't know about it, that which the SEEN obscures with their propaganda machine. But the dreamspice was given to our ancestors as the key to divination, to the communion with the Rainbow Connection. That's the pure ancestors the SEEN like to go on about: but these ancestors preceed everyone, English, Asian, the Khanate, whatever ... the pure ancestors were there at the creation of the world, man, and were in communion with the Real Rainbow Connection man ... that's why the dreamspice exists, it was their technology for that, dig? The cult of the SEEN has hidden this with their surface interpretation, hidden the meaning of the Connection behind their fucked up politico–genetic fantasies of world domination. They are a religion gone psychotic, moo–cow. Or else a politics that will justify itself whatever by whatever means it deems necessary, including those it would probably classify as 'cultural'."

The FNA is taking full effect now. You are aware that a drug, a chemical, is having an effect on your mind, your thoughts. It is an artificial, external thing that runs through your blood, your brain, your being. But it's a medicine. You feel yourself purged of – not the poison, but the *imprecision* of the SEEN cultists.

"Yes, you can see now," nods the master. "It is a surface they insist upon. The dreaming makes it precise."

You spend the next year with the Freezone, following their teaching. Hal Age says this is the true teaching of Desmond. He says that the fundamentalist SEEN are the wayward: they don't understand Desmond, refusing to peel the skin of the fruit of the Doctrine, hating the taste of truth's wine, only reading the superficial, never penetrating the beyond.

Why did you agree to join? The initial meeting is a total revelaton. The FNA made more sense of everything in four hours than a year at the Clearing Centre could ever had.

Hal Age has confirmed your still heartfelt belief in the Doctrine of Desmond, but also your supposedly contradictory doubts of the SEEN movement.

The first lesson was simply that Desmond died a long time ago.

Hal Age was never a renegate apostate. He was, in fact, Desmond's main scribe, and the first convert to the original SEEN. He knew the truth about Desmon's words, as no one was closer to that Source of knowledge than Hal Age. And for that reason, the other elders of the SEEN were jealous. It was widely expected that Hal Age would succeed Morris eventually. But when the Seer died, the elders were fast to use politics to bring a majority against Hal, convincing the followers that Desmond was still alive through use of computer graphics and special effects. Threats and more than threats banished Hal Age and the loyal forevers into a blizzard of lies and slander. The Freezone are what remains of the true believers.

You live in a log cabin with two Russian converts: the Freezone is actually bigger here in Russia than the SEEN is in Norn Albion. The converts are enthusiastic and ernest. The biggest contrast about the Freezone is the comradery and freedom to discuss whatever you want with your neighbour, without the constant monitoring of a Control.

However, amongst all this is a deeper tension. The fear of violent reprisal. That's the reason why Hal Age is wheelchair bound: he was shot in the spine by SEEN fanatics. Since Hal's depature, the elders instated a core violent paramillitia, called the Dread K, whose primary agenda is the fervent defense and conquest of their faith against and over all other systems. And this includes the Freezone.

Hal Age put it like this to a group of you, one Ourobsday evening. "There are secrets we tell here, secrets known since the beginning of days. And now we release these secrets, like caterpillars turning into butterflies of truth, or like the single seed in the soil of the earth transforms into a flower of understanding, blossoming toward the sunlight."

He paused.

"And what do the ignorant do? At the sight of this single butterfly, this first bud of May, they have killed, killed, killed. And will continue to kill, as our truth suddenly becomes apparent. But we will defeat them through wisdom, not through violence. Wisdom is often construed as trickery in the past. So let it be in the example to come. Let it be known: WE SHALL FIGHT THE Dread K IN THE SNOW, IN THE FOREST WE SHALL CONFRONT THEM. WITH OUR WEAPON OF TRUTH, WE ARE READY FOR THEM!"

Another year, another commune. From the outsider's perspective, it would look like you are wandering aimlessly between religions, a lost soul who has found no meaning. But you know that this is a progression. Without the SEEN, without Felicity, you would still be an average norm, going with the flow of society, whose purpose in life is simply to find a good job with the party and a husband able to lift you from the poverty of your idealist parents. Then that veil in turn was lifted though: for Hal Age and the Freezone are the real SEEN, the SEEN beyond the SEEN. They observe the same rights of communion, the women abide by the same rules of modesty in dress (albeit the headscarves are now optional). All laws – both relating to lifestyle and meta–lifestyle – derive solely from the RC Doctrine. But it is with living breath that they read and understand the text. The text got you to join the SEEN communion in the first place, inspired you to follow. But in a way, the communion and the centre killed that initial inspiration with their reading, a reading where the text and its words are dead and all that remains is the political struggle against the Party. A purely material descent into the same obsession with genetics that plagues the Martian Communism.

"There may have been a Khan. There may not have been. Historically. The point is not historical, it is parable. Here at the Freezone, we will help you to isolate the Khan within. But then the SEEN mainstream will tell you the Khan must be eliminated. We say no: the Khan is a necessary part of our being, a precondition for our spiritual development in fact. You just need to learn to control that mongol force inside yourself."

Hal Age teaches the Freezone about his circuit model of consciousness. "These are the real levels, the levels the Clearing Centre obscured. Level 1 is our condition within the world: it is epitomized by being a party member in society. Level 2 is organized religion and worship: this is where the SEEN are, but also where the Party itself is. Its drug is alcohol. Level 3 is the path of thought: it is where rational philosophers and theologions have walked. Its drug is the dreamspice. Level 4 is the Freezone, where we all exist right now, the zone of total freedom of the mind, deprogramming to reach the zenneth of that path to understanding. Its drug is the Doctrine itself."

Wow, you think.

You are awoken from your sleep by the hard kick of a boot against your scull. The Freezoner women are screaming. A man is shouting "stop please", you can smell burning, maybe it's the farm as the cattle are braying. It's the fucking police. You reach for the gun you keep under the bed, and aim it at a stormtrooper.

But Hal Age freezes time with the wave of his hand. The policeman's reactive grimace is utterly frozen, his baton paused a millisecond before landing upon you.

"No fighting! Remember this was meant to be," he insists.

You are startled by the situation, but have seen him work enough magic for you to focus on the danger at hand. "But they are destroying everything."

"Their persecution is necessary. The answer can only be delivered ... after the question has been raised, no matter how violently."

Turn to page 136 to follow Hal's orders.
Turn to page 134 to follow your gut instinct and shoot.

You pull the trigger at the policeman in front of you. Hal shouts – "No!" – but it is too late.

Your face is covere in a thick warm spurt of blood. Two other police are about to fire back, but something takes over and you effortlessly take them out.

You pull the helmet off the officer and are shocked to see Felicity's face. Hal is laughing at you, but you don't see what is funny.

The dead police officers get up and take off their helmets. One of them is your Clearing officer.

Hal removes his mask: he is Desmond Morris.

You understand now. You are still in Edinburgh. This whole thing has been a training exercise.

"And you blew it," replies Hal/Desmond, reading your thoughts. It's going to take a lot more work before you reach level 7 sister".

The End

Control, in particular, still haunts your dreams, and you tell the doctor so.

“We need to make Control manifest, so you can confront him,” declares the doctor. ”We’re going to give you a new drug, FNA D–07. You’re lucky, you get to do it legally. It’s becoming quite the hit in the clubs, where it is more commonly known as dream-spice. It’s still experimental, and so illegal outside of institutions such as ours. But reports indicate that it has been known to free up all kinds of – what we in the profession refer to as – mental glue. It keeps you on track, but sometimes a bit of self–awareness is in order, y’know babe?”

You take the FNA, and almost instantly fall back. You first become acutely aware that the doctor is filming you, recording your reaction to the drug, presumably for his medical research. You feel quite indignant about this. You’re not some kind of damn ginea pig, after all! You are about to tell him so, when you see he dissolves into ... wallpaper. And his camera ... it becomes ... a woman. A woman, wearing a veil, a nikab in the style worn only in the Islamic Republic of America.

Wow, you think.

Turn to page 149.

You awake, foully, to a pot of stinking feces thrown over you.

Get up you freak scum! A policewoman screams. She kicks you in the face, you lose several front teeth.

You are too stunned to react in any way apart from pissing like an animal in fear. Hal Age, protect me!

They torture you. For the next 6 months they regularly humiliate you, shit on you, bleed on you, cut, burn, rape in unending number of deviant cruelties. Screams echo throughout the prison, day and night, a never ceasing mantra of the soul's gradual grinding down into shattered shards, splinters of piteous numbing pain. You are injected with stimulants and shown images of your family, your friends, your old life at College, but always with some kind of twisted ending: your mother eating your pet cat for breakfast, Felicity being fucked by Penelope and Macy with Desmond Morris himself watching on in satanic amusement. And when you can't take it any more, they show you a video of Hal Age, beaten and broken, standing before a mock government trial, admitting his role in the terrorist bombings, begging forgiveness from the Ourobus. It can't be true!

But then true beauty was shown to you the week prior to his execution. You sat behind bars in your narrow cage, the sad prayers of some of the more determined prisoners muttering their devotion to the RC. The interrogators have tortured and beaten you down: nothing more than nervous systems fucked spiritually, destitute and prostitute. But for some reason, they permit this little bit of devotion to the Doctrine. It's the one moment of recollection, where you may gather the echos of what you were, where you can recover your being in contemplation. And you grasp these moments like a drowning man breathes his last lungfull of air. You anticipate with freakoutdread: what do they plan to do, eventually, with this last vestage of your selfhood?

Suddenly, appearing both within and without your mind, a radiant figure, so external that at once this illusion becomes shattered. It is he: Hal Age, walking free, down the coridoor, outside the bars!

"Master!" You cry tears upon joyful tears. "You escaped!"

"Oh, that's the question, my dear. That's the question: how do we escape?" he laughs. "I know how. Because I can see the Real, and the Real is me. And so tonight I will use this gnosis to release all prisoners, because gnosis is release."

You now stand outside of your cell. As you run after him, he makes the following speech, motioning a hand here and there, opening the doors for all, a rising, cheering rebellion of prisoners: "The prison is of the mind, indisputably. Take this to those antagonists who profess I say something else: the prison is of my mind. The jail is what the inmates call the Real, the HAQ. My realisation: I am the jailer and the warden. But that is not what the Touched of Ages call Divinity. What lies beyond the Real: that is the Truth, that is the Beloved Lover, that is the Source of the hyperdimensional infusion of perfume, perfume upon the cheek of the earthly mistress, the source of the miracles of inner reflection. Know this, the miracle which came before me: I am simply a minor gnostic!"

So it is done: somehow the guards are now in the prison cells, and the prisoners are outside. They quickly commandere the aircraft and prepare to escape to a safe rebel enclave protected by the African State.

You are to go with them, but then notice Hal Age is sitting, crossed legged, back in the prison courtyard.

"Master, we must leave soon, as the reinforcements will soon return."

"I have escaped, what need have I then for retreat? I have found stillness unfolded, so what need have I to move from this place?"

You understand, and so stay with him: as he is with the One, so are you are with Him, and it will be your martyrdom too. So turn now to page 142.

Else, leave behind your master. You don't understand his last speech completely, but surely he knows all, and so you should go and preach his message with the freed. Turn to page 140.

You run to the helicoper. As you climb abord, the wind blowing your blonde tresses romantically in the breeze, you take one look back at your saviour, still sitting, lotus position, at the centre of the prison.

The inmate and the warden.

"The inmate and warden," exhales Felicity, your publisher, tapping the draft of the manuscript, glancing appreciatively – and ever so flirtateously, the way she does in that older–wiser Mrs Robinson way of hers – "Fantatic shit. Will totally corner the New Age market of the bookstores for Ourobusmonth."

"Glad you like it," you reply, accepting the dreamspice spliff.

You tour the book festivals. You remember one time, a quite dishy looking longhaired guy asked:

"I mean – far out, so his Oneness is Oneness with Language, right?"

"Yes, I suppose that's one way of putting it."

"So, the salvation is transcendent of language?"

"I'm not sure, to be honest." Your trademark laconic patter. Light titters from the audience. "I mean, at the risk of appearing fatuous, trascendence is a term applied in opposition to a unity with the Other, and my point is that oneness is itself is an impossibly immanent aspect of language. It is language, in a way, just as woman is. It can't be escaped, if we are to talk about oneness, because we talk simultaneously about transcendence. Y'know? I can't say: other than language – we are the inmates and the warder of language, of our realities. But on the other hand, there is a oneness with the language itself, not a transcendent oneness, nor an immanence of the Other, but rather a oneness with the Divine word that was planted within. And this embracing occurs through the immanence of speech. The amazing thing is that, at the centre of us all, at the centre of our being above and beyond and behind all stations, there runs the Divine Breath, providing the key to the puzzle, the means to pass through the eye of this needle because it *is* the eye of the needle, resplendent and necessary as it is."

“Where you get the inspiration for this shit, girl?!” your interviewer gasps, astounded.

“Wikipedia, honey, wikipedia.”

The audience laughs and applaudes in amusement.

The End

He guides you through the levels, to the 5th level: enlightenment itself. You lose your selfhood. You are, now, finally, what you are.

The soldiers return and place you both in cells again, but now you understand and feel no fear, as they peirce you, negate you, for their negation is the negation of unfolding. Of course the negation is more violent and frenzied, like the waves of an ocean – do the waves understand that the sea is a sea of love? But yes, they are really angry, because they don't understand what happened to the other prisoners.

"They were freed, by the grace of my lord: freed by the unfolding of the Real!"

"Fucking cunt's lost her fucking mind."

Blood over your vision.

As the interrogators beat and torture you with renewed viciousness, all you feel is love to them. Love to everything. Because love is everything. What is this beating, from offender to victim, if not just the underside of the waves whose motion purifies the perfection of insight?

And then one day they release you, wheelchair bound, and you find yourself at Hal Age's execution. It is full of nerdy computer science students. They cheer as the hangman leads him up to the gallows.

"What is important for the ecstatic is for the One to reduce him to oneness. Your action today unites the One and the Opposers together against myself and so bear witness to the Oneness of all."

You call out to him: "What is love?" He answers: "You will see it today, tomorrow, and the day after tomorrow."

And the People hang him that day, burned him the next day and threw his ashes to the wind the day after that. "This is love," Hal Age says. His legs are cut off and he smiles, saying "I used to walk the earth with these legs, now there's only one step to heaven, cut that if you can."

And when his hands are cut off he paints his face with his own blood.

"Why is he doing this?" the people ask.

"I have lost a lot of blood, and I know my face has turned yellow, I don't wish to appear pale–faced before my wedding day."

And the people throw his body into the river. The soldiers are aghast when they see that the blood rises in the water, spelling out a word:

TRUTH

Your parents push your wheelchair back to the waiting car, and you are weeping. Weeping tears of joy.

The End

You complete your exams and feel reasonably confident about the outcome.

But a few weeks later you receive terrible news. It's a letter from college: your scholarship has been suspended due to inappropriate behaviour.

Penelope decided a groveling apology wasn't enough. Like most Eugenics, she knows no compassion: she would have known that you could never afford college without the scholarship.

You return to work at the local canned soup factory with your mother and sister. At nights, the only relief from the burden of your daily toil is the sound of the Rainbow Connection record you bought on the way back from college, that fateful day, now already a whole life away. But of course, all this lasts less than 2 years, at which point, the universe is destroyed.

The End

Yes, this diamond differance, this lovemaking of the couple within your mind. This endless chase. This is the organism–orgasm, this is the Cyborgwittgenstein, this is ∀–space. Feared by those generations who preceded the age of exploration. But you do not fear it, for you are the modern journeywoman.

The Rainbow Connection are singing:

flying above the shore
she thinks she'd like to have some more
below the unseen
that's where we've all been

The singer on stage, not Desmond Morris, but a woman, veiled in nikab, the style of the Islamic Republic of America, she sings, motionless, holding on to the microphone as if she grasps the key to life itself. That's the sense of the scene anyway, phrased in the simple 4 dimensions of space and time: you *feel* this rather than *see* it, so to speak, like someone might absentmindedly feel a breeze against their cheek, because right now you are just breathing the incense that is pumping out from the smoke machine and wow y'know it's like you're in a cloud or something.

The singer removes her veil.

house of angels
psychonautic
bionautic future–tastic
hold two symbols
blue elastic
songs and dreams and golden plastic

You look into her face, directly. Yes, she is the Wise: the culmination and release.

Turn to page 148.

There is a crowd again with you, no longer that teacher's circle: in fact, many more than the circle. And they are dancing around you, jostling you, sweat and dreamspice in the air. And the music is getting louder.

And your mind is free. And you are dancing too.

Back at that concert, the moment after your vision of Desmond speaking to you.

"What the hell just happened," you shout wide eyed at the girl next to you. She looks at you quizzically, licks her florescent lips. "Why, Lightshow, of course." She nods her head to the beat in quarter time. "You're new to the Connection aren't you? That's great! Your first Lightshow girl! Far out!" She winks at you, turns back to face the band and starts to dance again. She looks up at the violent paroxysms of the light show and laughs happily. She blows her whistle ear–piercingly loud in time to the music.

And you know what she is talking about. Now you know: almost on the verge of complete obedience, a totalitarian violence of your worst kind, you are rescued right here and now and you know that you are rainbow connected.

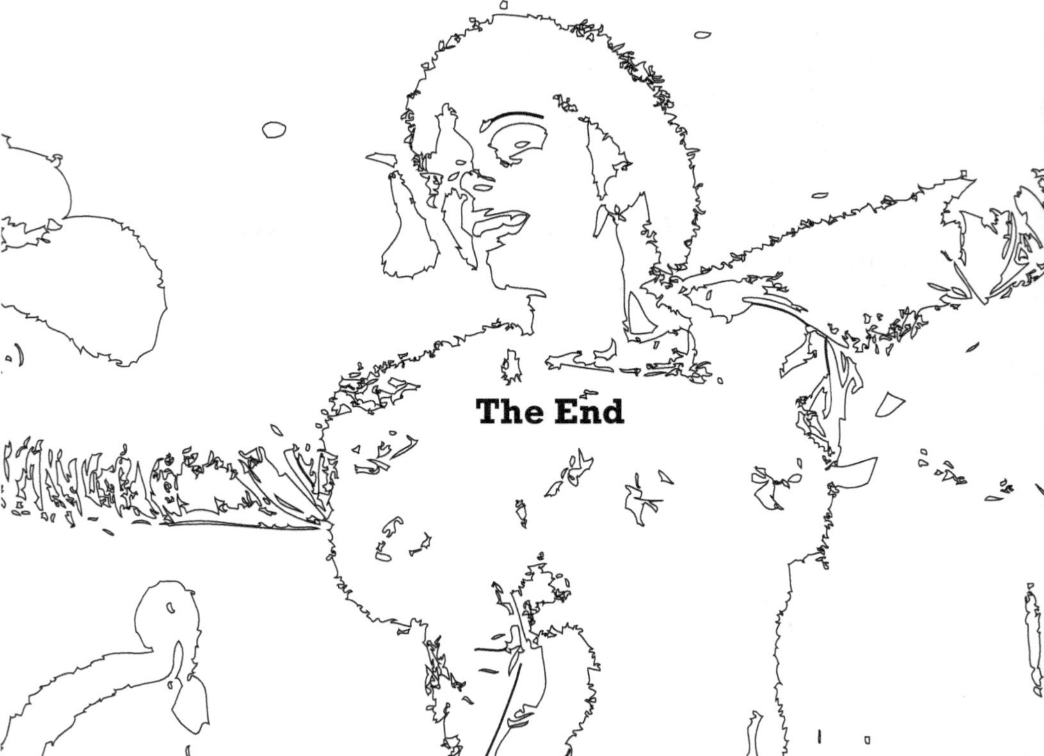

The End

You leave the auditorium along with the other spectators. "I'll just go powder my nose," says Felicity, heading to the bathroom queue.

You enter the cloakroom to retrieve your things. That was one wierd play. What the hell is that Desmond writer guy smoking? You are surprised he got backing from the Arts Council to put on something so psychedelic and experimental, particularly in this economic climate, must have been costly hiring that celebrity supermodel in the lead role and all those Holywood stars in a merely supporting cast, but apparently the main sponsor simply really digs on absurd theatre, everything from Ionescu to the Ta'vram Beth Cho nonsensical players of Alpha Centauri to the Quantum Fairy Sufi Heralds. If *it* is experimental, then that is where, apparently, the president's son wants *it* to be.

One final misturn. One final possible dead ending.

And you are snatched from it all, by the love. Misturns are of our own making: misturns are human and finite. The demiurge, the president, Desmond, Hal Age, every signifier who would have assumed that role: the demiurge is the master in the lovemaking, and the demiurge was you all along. But the Love, that was never in doubt: the Love is the Absolute Light, filtered into our reality as the light from the heavens. It *really* is like a pin–prick in the fabric of the universe, this source of light, this fusion internal. This primal reaction is more than a metaphor. It is the energy closest to that of the beginning, when it was all joined up. The measurement of physics is, in this sense, the measurement of reality.

But unlike the reality of physics, your life moves toward this *backwards*, through thought, speech, action. Through this diamond dialectic, this lovemaking, this road of turns, all of which you are wholly responsible for. You have determined your deviation: it is to be the determiner.

But a Loved determiner ... until ...

The End

Wow, what a trip. You wake up from your dream, disoriented. In some strange room. In a foreign hotel. Oh yes, you're off at the conference. Of course.

Fuck, should go easy on the dreamspice diamond. It's legal in this country, so you couldn't help do a bit when offered last night. But you haven't touched the stuff since your PhD and you're really getting too old for drugs.

You head to the shower and rehearse your speech in your mind. The conference isn't much fun, but you are invited speaker.

Promoting your book, "The Genetic Optimisation of Religion".

The End

She removes her veil, slowly, and as she does so it feels, literally, like a kind of veil is being removed from you, uncovering the very cells of your being, so that, by her action, your molecular nature is somehow recreated and re–formed. You now understand what the mystics refer to when they speak of entering a higher plane of reality.

"Be not afraid, for I am the Source," she says.

And you recognize her. But can't remember where you met.

"Some people call me Time, the foundation of selfhood. Some call me the Proof. Some call me Wisdom. But it might be more accurate to call me the Kiss of Personal Time, the Comfort of the Proof that reflects the Truth of Time descending from above. But enough of introductions, let's get straight to business.

"I am the hand turning from Left into Right. I am the agency, the meaning–as–use. You are granted my presence: but the choices you alone make construct your selfhood, construct your own becoming, finalise the flower, champion the choice, determine your own deviation."

And suddenly you get it. The mellifluous monologue pierces your heart with the burning sword of Truth, and you feel reborn!

"Our Timeline can be inauthentic or authentic. The philosophers have called this cowardly or heroic. But we call it guided or misguided by the Light that emerges in descent. A mastery of Time. If you do not possess mastery of Time, you go along, as they say, with the flow, and your choices are random, if not always precisely a statistical median of the choices made by the others, still stochastic and quantum in essence. But God does not play dice with the universe. If you possess mastery of Time, then you make the right choices at the right moment. The sinners of the world are those who are given the gift, but then mess up, given the pegs to keep the tent stable, but then abuse stabilisation to form fascism, are given the secret knowledge of the higher heavens, but then cut the ears of the cattle, a defacement of the possibilities to level them upon a single plateau that totalizes. Is this cowardice? Depends on your perspective. It is certainly bad timing.

"But there is Mercy for those without Time, as there is Grace for those with Time, because all retribution is one of balance. Retribution is restitution.

"How to gain mastery of Time, that is the question I am sure is on the tip of your tounge."

She smiles at you. "That itself is a choice, because choices spell out a logical line of flight, a differential delight, a curvacious clue, a proof of profundity and luminous limit. You may proceed through following me through this door of the left, the dangerous door of speech where we might find the garden or meet immediate death. Or you may leave me aside and focus your mind on the love that you know rests inside."

Turn to page 119 if you follow her.
Turn to page 116 if you manage to focus your mind alone.

LATER ... some hours after the agitation meeting, at Celcius' hotel room (ooh, whatagiveaway!) ...

"So it's clear. Their plot must be uncovered and disarmed," you share a post–coital joint with your new lover.

"Yes. You saw just one of their tricks, their prototype mind control technique, at the Rainbow Connection Lightshow of your university days. They are years more powerful than that now, with respect to group hallucination for the Gnostic anti–evolutionary cause. You might say they have infinity on their side, in fact." Celcius' tone is serious.

"But what can be done?"

"Well, let me put it this way. Life is a Rhizome, not a rooted tree. Lines extend, lines in bifircation, a breaking apart and ... a joining. Check this out, I'm branching into fiction now, writing a dramatic version of what I've been going on about in my agitation propaganda work."

"Show me."

"It's all about a lady spy who is working for the People to rid society of anti–evolutionist threat. There's this bit I am especially proud of where she's going to destroy the cult for good. She's magnificent, a true patriot.

"Here. Let me show you the page."

He hands you the manuscript to his book. It's all written in second person, like those children's books from ages ago. As you read it, the dreamspice seriously kicking in, you become intoxicated with the truth that the "she" of the book is you, wearing a military uniform.

"Doppleganger," his white teeth in wide grin, stark contrast against tanned skin.

The End

And she appears again, for you know her in one strand of this puzzle as certainly as you don't know her in another. A voice of pure white in the perfumed darkness, a comforting sensuality descending upon you, reaching out, calling you out to the ocean.

You step out to her extended hand and now you both walk, walking upon the waters.

The moon is overhead, ripples of its reflection render your spirit drunk.

And your heart beats faster: *this is the silent kiss.*

As you walk further towards the horizon, you reach the sandy banks of land and the light of the sun begins to dawn. And you see two figures, one on the left, it is Celcius, but not exactly Celcius, something distorted about his face, can't quite discern what. And on the right, a figure in a full veil, but you know somehow that this is Desmond Morris.

Turn to page 119.

What have you won?

Have you reached all the possible endings of The Rainbow Connection?
Use the following table to mark off all your lines of flight.

Page	*Ending*	
58	*End up running a model agency.*	☐
62	*Engage in the final battle.*	☐
80	*Become the leader of the nation along the edge of time.*	☐
84	*Comprehend the inner meaning of this book.*	☐
86	*Comprehend the outer meaning of this book.*	☐
100	*Tricked by the snakelady into strange psychic politics.*	☐
107	*Kill the Dread K.*	☐
125	*Encounter the terror of replication.*	☐
134	*Disobey Hal Age and mistime with your action.*	☐
141	*Become a successful author.*	☐
143	*Witnessed Hal Age's martyrdom.*	☐
144	*Back to the soup factory.*	☐
146	*Become fully rainbow connected.*	☐
147	*Exit the theatre and reach a final dead end.*	☐
148	*Remember the popular science writer.*	☐
151	*Sleep with Celcius.*	☐

Importantly, there are also two other endings within this book – an infernal closed loop and the ultimate **Angelic** ascent into the ultimate Victory. We do not give the page numbers to these but wish you fun and games in attempting to locate them.

About the author.

Herman U. Ticz, Ph.D. is the director of the Central Asian Psychoanalytic Institute, dividing his time between its twin ashrams in London and Almaty. He has pioneered research into the realisation of the human body through modern technology. His minked and blinged out oriental lover **sally d** is an international meta–model and hyperwood film star. Ticz is an enthusiastic exponent of Tantric Tailorism, Vinology and Polyamory, and is often followed by an admiring crowd of sisters, cousins and aunts, most of them imaginal and some of them cats (and all of them a Tablet). This is his second Determine Your Own Deviation™ novel.

About the illustrator.

Purdy Ranger has been working as an illustrator and graphic designer for over 15 years. Lithe, athletic, blond with penetrating steel grey eyes, both a perfect 10 and, paradoxically for a mimetic artist, a devout Muslim, she graduated with distinction in illustration from Central Saint Martins College of Art and Design and is, by her own admission, a performative fictional assemblage of the unconscious visual code that operates just above the internet, like a spectre.

About the author

www.ingramcontent.com/pod-product-compliance
Lightning Source LLC
Chambersburg PA
CBHW070553180626
46817CB00005B/1821

* 9 7 8 1 4 4 5 7 3 5 3 8 2 *